GLARE ICE

A CLAIRE WATKINS MYSTERY

Mary Logue

TYRUS
BOOKS

Also by Mary Logue

◆

BLOOD COUNTRY
DARK COULEE

Published in electronic format by
TYRUS BOOKS
an imprint of F+W Media, Inc.
10151 Carver Road
Blue Ash, Ohio 45242
www.tyrusbooks.com

eISBN 10: 1-4405-3292-3
eISBN 13: 978-1-4405-3292-4

POD ISBN 10: 1-4405-5403-X
POD ISBN 13: 978-1-4405-5403-2

This is a work of fiction. Names, characters, corporations, institutions, organizations, events,
or locales in this novel are either the product of the author's imagination or, if real, used
fictitiously. The resemblance of any character to actual persons (living or dead) is entirely
coincidental.

This work has been previously published in print format by:
Walker Publishing Company, Inc.
Print ISBN: 0-8027-3371-9

Peter, it comes back to you again and again

I would like to thank Pat Anderson, Lund fire chief, for his information on ice-rescue training, and Christie Rundquist for talking to me about emergency medical technicians (EMTs). Much appreciation to my careful readers: Elizabeth Gunn, Marianne and Jim Mitchell, and Mary Anne Collins-Svoboda. Thanks to Jane Chelius, my agent, and Michael Seidman, my editor, and the rest of the crew at Walker. Special thanks to John Martinez for the beautiful covers of my books. To Pete Hautman I owe much love and gratitude for the right word at the right moment, and many good meals along the way.

For the ice and the river under it are never still for long. Again and again throughout this long winter, water will find its way into the open, welling up from a seam in the ice, and spreading over the existing surface of ice and snow to freeze again in a perilous sheet. The wind will bring its dry snow to polish the new ice and turn it into a great slick and glare.

—John Haines, *The Stars, the Snow, the Fire*

GLARE ICE

The phone rang in the early-morning hours as the first hint of light lifted over the eastern bluffline. Claire turned in her bed, opened one eye, and looked at the invading phone.

It rang again. She reached out a hand, grabbed the receiver, and at the same time pushed herself up in bed. She held the phone to her ear and listened. A faint sound, a hum. Claire knew there was a word you were supposed to say, a special word, and then she remembered it. "Hello."

Nothing.

Claire shook her head. She was going to be mad if it was one of those computer calls where they didn't start talking right away. But so early in the morning?

"Hello. Anyone there?" Claire asked.

This time she heard something. A squeak, breath being pulled deeply into lungs, let out in a shiver.

"Hello?"

Then she heard a sob, like a wave breaking along a shore.

"Can I help you?"

Weeping now. Gulping weeping, no chance for words to come out.

"I'll hold on. Try to calm down and tell me what I can do."

That brought it on harder—horrible wrenching sobs coming from the belly. Claire could tell it was a woman.

Claire held tightly to the receiver, wanting to yell into it, but restrained herself. She wanted to know who was calling, didn't want to scare her off the line.

"I'm still here."

The sobs subsided. More quick gulps of breath.

"Can you tell me who you are?"

A woman's shaky voice started, "I can't . . . What he did to me . . ." Quick intake of air. The phone clicked down on that end.

Claire felt her whole body tense with anger. She couldn't stop the woman from hanging up on her. "Who is this?" she asked to empty air.

But the connection was cut. The waning night hung quiet around her. Claire found herself leaning forward in her bed, holding the dead phone in her hands as if she could bring it back to life.

1

As Claire dressed for the cold November weather, she thought about the oncoming winter season. This time of year she always felt positive about it, energized by it. But she knew that she would reach a point in the middle of the deep cold when she would dream of bright sun and beating-down warmth. So far this November had been breaking records for low temperatures. They had already been subzero a couple nights. The white lace of frost covered her window and made it difficult to see out.

She and Meg had lived in Fort St. Antoine for over a year. This would be their second winter. She intended to enjoy it more than she had her first. Maybe she would buy them both snowshoes for Christmas. She still hoped to finish the quilt she was stitching for Meg's bed. It was a simple block design, and all she had left to sew was the border.

Thanksgiving was coming, and they would be having it in their own house. Last year they had gone to spend it with her husband's parents. Because of Steve's recent death, it had been a very depressing affair. Claire had managed not to cry, but Steve's mother had left the dinner table weeping before the pumpkin pie was served.

This year would be different. Rich was going to be with them. Just the three of them. She planned to cook a turkey with mashed potatoes, gravy, wild rice, and of course, pumpkin pie. They would have leftovers for a week, but they would have a real Thanksgiving.

Reaching into her closet, she pulled out her mother's old Bemidji woolen plaid jacket with fringe on the sleeves. She tied her dark hair back and then pulled on a lovely hand-knit natural wool cap that she had bought at the local art fair.

Meg looked up from the television cartoons and gave her the once-over. "You look like a lumberjack, Mom."

"Thanks, sweetie. That's just the word of encouragement I needed to go out into the day."

"A cute lumberjack." Meg's eyes brightened, and she asked, "Hey, Mom, can we have a fire tonight?"

"Probably," Claire had answered as she stepped out the door. Promise nothing. Meg remembered everything and would hold her to all promises. It was better to be vague but hopeful.

Walking down the hill from her house to Main Street, Claire could see all the way across Lake Pepin to the Minnesota shore. Lake Pepin was a thirty-three-mile-long, two-mile-wide bulge in the Mississippi River, which flowed by Fort St. Antoine. There was a cloudy film floating on the water like a cataract forming in a blue eye. Along the shoreline a wide band of ice filigree shone in the sun.

The water that she could see had turned a deep steel blue. Finally, the lake was starting to freeze over. Meg would be so happy. She could hardly wait to try out her skates again this year and asked every day if there was any ice on the lake yet.

The weather was continuing to be very cold for late November, five degrees this morning when she had checked the thermometer on the porch. The radio had promised a high of only fifteen. No snow had fallen yet, but it was in the air.

The trees stood stark and naked. This hill had been so lush in summer. Claire liked the woods revealing themselves, though, the branches reaching bare toward the sky The land had moved to neutral and had a spareness to it that she found elegant.

She loved walking down to the post office to pick up her mail first thing in the morning on Saturdays. She wished she could do it every day, but during the week, work got in the way.

The shrill screech of a hawk overhead reminded her of the call she had gotten a couple of mornings ago. The sobbing. From the little the woman had said, Claire wondered if it was a case of domestic abuse.

She had not been able to go back to sleep; instead she tried to track down where the call had come from. She had called the operator, but found out that she lived in one of the few parts of the country that didn't have caller ID. Without that, there seemed to be no way for the phone company to track down a local call. All she knew was that it had been a local call.

The next day at work, she checked with everyone to see if there had been any emergency calls reporting household strife, anything involving a woman. Nothing. No battered women had showed up at any of the local hospitals or shelters. She had tried to let it go. The slight possibility that it had been a prank call occurred to her, but she doubted it. The woman's weeping still haunted her.

Claire stopped into Stuart Lewis's bakery, Le Pain Perdu. The smell of fresh-baked bread made her mouth water. Stuart was pulling loaves of crusty bread out of the oven in the back. He was wearing a white apron and a Packers cap sat backward on his head. It was common knowledge in town that Stuart was gay, although he didn't particularly flaunt it. Rich and he were best friends, which had led to speculation in the past. Rich just laughed the suggestions off.

"Two French doughnuts, monsieur," she ordered after he had set down his load.

"Oui, madame." Stuart smiled and fished them out of the shelf with metal tongs. "Would you tell Rich that there's a poker game tomorrow night at Hammy's?"

"Sure. I'm seeing him tonight." Somehow it bothered her that Stuart was using her to pass on messages to Rich. He could pick up the phone and call him. She didn't see Rich every day of the week, and they weren't living together. Often they only got together a couple times during the week. She didn't like how much people had invested in them being a couple, but maybe she was making much out of nothing.

Stuart crossed his arms over his chest for a moment and asked, "Did you see the ice on the lake?"

"Yup, I suppose it'll be the big news in town today."

"Hey, it's either that or watching the paint peel off the village hall."

Claire strolled down the short street. It was too early for the other stores in town to be open. By ten o'clock cars would line the street, most sporting Minnesota license plates, ready to look at the antiques in the old restored buildings of this small river town. This early, it was mainly Fort St. Antoine citizens walking the streets, doing their morning chores.

Sven Slocum, a retired 3M executive who had moved down to Fort St. Antoine ten years ago, was out in front of his place sweeping leaves from the sidewalk. He kept his small house and yard immaculate. Yellow tulips cut from sheets of plywood lined the sidewalk; woodworking was just one of the many ways he kept busy in retirement. He had coffee with the other older men every morning at the Fort, and seemed to fit in to the small town.

"Howdy, Mrs. Cop," he hollered.

"Hi, there, Sven. A lovely day, don't you think?"

He stopped his sweeping for a moment and thought about it. "I'll take it."

Claire turned the corner and headed to the post office, which was tucked next to the bank. When she pushed open the door, a blond woman wearing a too-large green-and-gold

Packers jacket was standing with her back to Claire, opening her PO box. After pulling out a few envelopes, the woman turned quickly, nearly running into Claire.

Claire reached out to steady her and was struck by the damage visible on the woman's face: a nasty gash over one eye, a battered lip, and a large raw spot high on her cheekbone. Involuntarily, Claire gasped.

"Are you all right?" A slight hesitation—Claire saw an opening in the woman's eyes—then she ducked her head and pushed past Claire and out the door.

Claire watched her leave, then turned to catch the eye of the postmaster. Sandy Polanski shook her head.

"Who was that?" If anyone would know anything about the woman, it would be Sandy.

Sandy Polanski had been postmistress for over fifteen years. She looked like a down-to-earth Liza Minelli, with straight black hair cut in a bob. Her husband, Steven, whom everyone called Poly, was a plumber who knew the inner workings of most of the houses in the area, so between them they knew everything that was going on in the township. Sandy was forty years old, had lived in the county all her life, and had one of the most generous spirits Claire had ever met.

Sandy saw most everyone in town five days a week. She knew who was recovering from what operation, who was waiting for a check in the mail, whose grandchildren had been down to visit. She wasn't nosy, but she was there, consistent, every day, smiling behind the counter, pleasant, so people told her things.

"You don't know Stephanie Klaus? She's lived in town the last five or six months. Kind of keeps to herself. She's from Eau Claire, I think. Got a brother down in Winona. She lives in that blue house near the edge of town, toward Pepin."

"The one right on the highway?"

"Yeah, with the tire full of red petunias in the summer."

"I know which one you mean." Claire also remembered Stephanie from the art fair that was held in the park in the summer. Stephanie had shared a booth with a couple of other woman—all of their work had been weaving of some kind. Claire had looked at some of the rag rugs that Stephanie made, thinking to get one or two of them for her house. Maybe it was time to go ask Stephanie about them. "She looked awful. Do you know what happened to her?"

Sandy shook her head again. "No. She came in looking like that one time before. As I recall, it was right after she moved here. Looks like someone's beating her up."

"Looks that way."

"Can you do anything about it?"

"Not if she won't report him. I could try talking to her."

Sandy added, "He beat her up just bad enough so she looks like hell, but not bad enough so she'd report it."

"Those bruises look a few days old. Do you know when it happened, Sandy?"

"No." Sandy said, then thought for a moment. "Wait a minute. I did see her on Tuesday, and she was fine. But then I haven't seen her in here the rest of the week. She didn't come to get her mail either. It just piled up in her box."

Claire wondered if Stephanie had been the woman who had called her—the timing was right. She thought to ask something else that had been bothering her. "Do you think she knows who I am?"

Sandy laughed. "Claire, are you kidding? Everyone knows who you are. You're the only cop in town. And a woman to boot. You're big news around here."

Claire left the post office and looked down Highway 35. She could see the green jacket a few blocks down the road, moving slowly away. Stephanie Klaus. She was moving like she still hurt, like every step took a little out of her.

Claire thought again of the new ice forming over the lake. Like skin, a thin covering over a large body. And like skin, so easily broken.

✦

He had found her again.

Take another step down the sidewalk, Stephanie told herself. Get yourself home before you fall apart.

She felt her mind scramble with fear. It was hard for her to think straight when she had so much to avoid thinking about. It was hard to keep walking when her body ached to the core.

Jack would come again. He had promised her he would find her, and hurt her bad, if she told anyone. Next time it would be worse. A lot worse. He had been very clear about that. He had made her repeat it back to him. Then he had kissed her and held her breasts in his hands like they were two stones that he might smack together. She had said she would do anything that he wanted. She had meant it.

Her house was only four blocks from the post office, but it was a long walk. Her bones felt as if they had been cracked. She hadn't been out of the house since the beating. Maybe she should have waited another couple days. Took the doggone bruises so long to heal.

She thought of killing herself. Getting it over with. Doing it before he did it. Doing it right out in public. She would go down to Shirley's Bar outside of Nelson and take a pile of barbiturates with a few drinks, fall asleep in the dark corner of the bar. Wouldn't Shirley get a scare when she found her there, thinking she was just drunk and finding out she was a dead drunk?

Stephanie felt a laugh burble up inside herself, but resisted. Laughing led to crying. She didn't know why. Maybe it was just any emotion ripped her open and made her want to cry.

She had called in sick for the whole end of the week, but she would go back to work on Monday. She worked at W.A.G., the pet food factory near Red Wing. The bruises would be in their final stage, but she could put on plenty of makeup. No one much looked at her. They were so desperate for help that they would never fire her.

It had started out fine.

At first, she had even been glad to see Jack.

He seemed like he had changed. He told her she looked great. He said he missed her. He even went so far as to say he couldn't live without her. He brought flowers. He said he would never let her go.

Maybe it was her fault. She had tried to ask him some questions, to pin him down. He got mad and wouldn't answer.

Then she made the big mistake of telling him about Buck. That was it. He blew up. She didn't see it coming. His eyes changed. They turned evil, as if some deep darkness lying in wait inside of him was released by her words. He had asked her to tell him all about this new boyfriend.

When she saw what a mistake she had made and stopped talking, he had said what he always said: "I don't want to have to beat it out of you." And it had sounded the way it always sounded—the opposite of what he really meant.

Once they reached this point, she never knew what to do to stop him.

This time, she tried to touch him. She said, "Please, Jack. It can be so good with us."

He grabbed her wrist before she could touch him. He started bending her arm back. He said, "Until you ruin it."

He kept bending her arm.

She was afraid he would break it. She never knew whether she should scream at him or try to endure it. Whimpering sounds came out of her mouth. He let go of her suddenly, and she fell to the floor.

He laughed his cough laugh and then kicked her in the stomach.

She lay still, hoping that was it.

Then he told her to stand up. When she didn't move right away, he grabbed her arm and pulled her up. After slamming her against the wall, he moved in on her.

His face was contorted with rage. He became someone she didn't know. He looked like a demon, like a devil of anger.

He put his hands around her neck and began to choke her. She tried to get a wisp of air, and when it didn't come, she went into a total panic, slapping out at him, trying to get away.

The choking was the worst. He had only done that once before. She had thought he was going to kill her. It taught her that he could.

Just when she thought she would pass out, he let her go. Let her fall to the floor. She didn't move. Let him think she was dead. Maybe he would leave her alone then.

He walked away and looked out the window at the lake. Then he came back toward her and kicked her in the face. She screamed.

"You know what I can do," he said, standing over her.

When he was leaving, he said he would be back. She wondered when. Now that he had come to her house, he would do it again. He had told her there was a bond between them that was stronger than any other kind of love on Earth. There was no pattern to his anger. It made it harder not knowing what made it happen.

Once she had loved him so much that she didn't mind when he beat her. Every time he had promised her it would never happen again. Every time he had been so good to her afterward, it more than made up for it. But after he had choked her the first time, she had left him.

That was over a year ago.

She reached her house and climbed the stairs, then pushed open the front door to her house.

It smelled funky. Her house had turned into a pigsty this week. She hadn't done anything but moved from the bed to the couch. What was the use, when her world was going to be destroyed?

Stephanie sat down at her kitchen table and felt huge gulps of sobs pushing up inside her, trying to break out. She swallowed hard. Do something, she thought, anything rather than start crying again.

She stood and carried her coffee cup to the sink. The dishes were piled up until there wasn't any room to put another plate down. Time to do the dishes.

She cleared out the sink and piled the dishes on the counter. She ran the water until it was hot, so hot it scorched her hands. Then she poured some yellow liquid soap into it. The bubbles came. She sank her dirty dishes into the water. She washed the dishes and stood them up in the drying rack.

Stephanie had always liked washing dishes. Submerging her hands in the warm water felt good after her cold walk to town. After a hard day's work at the factory, it was about the only way she could get her fingernails clean. When she was finished with the dishes, she wiped down all the counters with her sponge. The kitchen was clean. It was a good start.

A bath. She needed a long, hot bath. She would wash her hair. She would put clean sheets on the bed.

Stephanie looked down at her hands. Short, stubby fingers. Plump and soft. They looked just like her mother's hands. She should never have told her mother where she was. Her mother had a soft spot for him. She always told him everything, even when she promised not to.

2

CAN smell pumpkin pie," Rich said as soon as he walked in
the door. He let himself in without even knocking.

Claire was surprised by how good it was to see him. He
had only been gone since Wednesday, driving a load of pheasants up to Alexandria in Minnesota, but it felt like longer. It
was the end of his busy season; he had frozen pheasants that
he would deliver to town through the holidays, but that was
the end of it.

He looked tired but happy, his dark hair falling in his eyes.
He was wearing a red plaid shirt with the sleeves rolled up,
jeans, and Red Wing boots. Pretty standard outfit for down
along the river, but she knew and loved the body that was under it all, lean and muscled, weathered in a good way.

Claire remembered, amused, that when she was twenty
she had worried about whether she would like men her age
when she was forty. At the time, she hadn't found older men
attractive. But of course, as she matured, so had her taste in
men.

Now when she looked at Rich, who was moving in on

fifty, she loved what she saw: the touch of gray in the hair at his temples, the wrinkles that accentuated his moods, laugh lines around the mouth, eyes that crinkled with delight when he was happy, and even the thought lines that appeared in his forehead when he was puzzled. She loved them all. She found young men in their late teens and early twenties surprisingly blank, unformed-looking.

She walked out to greet him. "Good to see you," she said and stood in front of him. He pulled her in closer, and they kissed deeply for a moment. Then she heard footsteps coming down the stairs, and her daughter flung herself into the room.

"Rich, guess what?"

Claire and Rich pulled apart, and Rich bent down and hoisted the young girl on his hip. "What, my pumpkin pie?"

Meg turned and glared at Claire. "Mom, did you tell him?"

"Tell him what? I haven't said a thing to him."

Meg yelled, "I made you a pumpkin pie."

"My favorite."

"I thought apple was your favorite."

"I stand corrected. My second favorite. But my first favorite for the month of November."

"Because of Thanksgiving."

"You got it."

"Mom helped."

"Good plan. Let her think she's needed," Rich teased.

Meg squirmed down and grabbed his hand. "I want to show you something in my room."

Claire decided it was time to step in. "Later. He's going to be here all evening. Let Rich relax for a moment. Besides, he's my boyfriend, and I want to talk to him too."

"Yeah, but Mom—"

"No yeah-but-Moms right now. You go and set the table, please."

The evening was pleasant. Claire watched with pleasure as Rich cleaned his plate of pork chops, mashed potatoes, and steamed kale. Meg proudly brought out the pumpkin pie and even cut it with a little help. Big blobs of whipped cream were plopped on top, and they all declared it the best they had ever eaten.

"I didn't know pumpkin pie could be so good, Mom."

"It's always better if you make it yourself."

"Then you can trust everything that's in it, right?"

Claire laughed and thought what an odd thing that was for Meg to say. "Do you sometimes worry about what's in your food?"

"Well, sometimes I worry about the school lunches."

They all laughed.

"Speaking of food, can I talk to you about Thanksgiving?" Rich said.

Claire's heart sank. Was he going to tell her he couldn't make it? "Sure."

"Well, I was just wondering if there was any chance of my mother having it with us."

"Of course. What happened? I thought she was going to some friends."

"They canceled on her."

Claire couldn't believe they had progressed this far already. She would be meeting Rich's mother for the first time. The woman was coming to her house—talk about putting the pressure on. Rich's father had died a few years ago, and his mother lived in Rochester, Minnesota. He said he thought she moved there to be closer to the clinic, "just in case."

"Okay, let me ask you this. What do you need to eat for Thanksgiving?"

Rich cocked his head, puzzled. "What?"

"You know. Everyone has that special dish that makes or breaks it. Wild rice, green bean casserole with fried onion rings, cherry Jell-O with bananas and whipped cream. What's yours?"

Rich thought. "I guess it would have to be the chestnut dressing. My mom always makes chestnut dressing."

"Wow. That sure sounds exotic and rich. We better have your mom bring that, because it certainly isn't on my menu. And I meant to ask you—is it okay if we don't have pheasant?"

"More than okay. A big turkey is just what I want." Rich turned and looked at Meg. "And, of course, pumpkin pie."

Rich did the dishes while Claire settled Meg into bed, letting her read until she was sleepy because it wasn't a school night. "I want your light out by ten-thirty at the latest, you hear?"

"Is Rich staying over?" Meg whispered.

"I would guess so."

"Yes," Meg said and snuggled into her blankets.

Back downstairs, she found Rich lounging in front of the woodstove, a cup of coffee in his hands.

"I'm amazed you can drink that stuff and still sleep at night," she said.

"Well, I was planning on doing a little more than sleeping tonight."

"Maybe I should have some too." She sat down next to him, took his cup, and drank a couple sips.

He took the cup from her, put it down on the coffee table, and pulled her close for another kiss.

After a moment Claire pulled back far enough to be able to see his face. "Rich, when was the last time you hit someone?"

He looked at her, and a slow smile bloomed on his face. "You know, I can always count on you for romantic conversation."

"This is leading to something."

"I've no doubt of that. Let's see. I pounded Scotty Warden in sixth grade out back of the school. I slugged a guy in France when he tried to lift my wallet. That's about it. Disappointed?"

"Have you ever hit a woman?"

He put his hands on her shoulders. "Against my religion. Claire, what's going on? Are you having panic attacks again?"

"No, nothing like that. I'm trying to understand something. I hit a boy when I was in fifth grade. We were fighting over whether I tagged him out at first. I can't quite remember how it felt."

"Who won?"

"Nobody. I think we quit playing."

"What's this all about?"

"Do you know Stephanie Klaus?" Claire asked him.

"Sure. I know who she is. She lives out on the highway on my side of town. We've probably exchanged three sentences the whole time she's lived in town. I would say hi to her if I saw her on the street. That's about it."

"I think someone's been beating her up."

"Do you know who?"

"It's usually the husband, but since she doesn't have one, I'd guess it's the boyfriend."

"Is it a job for supercop?" he asked.

"That's what I'm trying to figure out."

Buck stood at the edge of the lake. The ice had formed weird ridges along the shoreline where the water had lapped up and frozen. Looked like it was at least four inches thick just out from shore. He thought of walking out onto it, but decided it might be wise to wait another day or two. There was supposed to be a hard freeze that night, drop down close to zero again. That would beef up the ice.

The lake didn't usually freeze up until the beginning of December, but the weather had been mighty mean lately. The *Farmer's Almanac* had predicted an early, cold winter. More snow than usual, too. He'd take it. He loved winter. It made him feel like a warrior every time he went out to start the car.

He kicked at the ice with his boots and then walked along. His dog, Snooper, was snuffling in the weeds. Probably found a dead fish or something. He had to watch that dog. Even though it was a tiny Pomeranian, it had the personality of a big dog and went at life with a lot of gusto. He had inherited Snooper when his grandmother had died. She had called the little dog Bitsy, but he hated that name. You give a dog a name like that, and he can't help but act like a wimp. Snooper fit him better, Buck decided.

He could hardly wait to get out on the ice. His skates were all ready to go. He had gotten them sharpened last week. He loved that he could go out, if the ice froze without too much snow on it, and skate the whole lake.

Even though he was big, he moved like lightning on ice skates. His dad had grown up on the range in northern Minnesota, and they put skates on their boys up there before they could walk.

Buck had grown up in the cities and played hockey all year long, skating late at night just to get ice time in the summer. He had played varsity his junior year. Went into his senior year one of the best, but got busted for smoking right before hockey season and kicked off the team.

It made him mad just thinking about it. He could have gotten a scholarship and been someone.

That was five years ago. Now all he did was work at W.A.G. Not much of a life—certainly no hopes for advancement—but he didn't mind the work.

Then there was Stephanie. Buck didn't know what to do about her. She made him feel like no other woman had ever made him feel: frustrated, helpless. He wished she would just listen and give in to him. But she had to resist. Maybe that's why he wanted her so bad.

He hadn't gone out with many women. Just had a hard time around them. But now he knew why. He had been waiting for the perfect one. Stephanie was perfect: beautiful, quiet, and kind. He had grown up in the Lutheran church, and they didn't have any saints, but if they did, she could be one.

Sometimes he felt like he didn't understand life. He had never been good at talking, but maybe he should try harder with Stephanie. If he sat on his hands and talked and tried to tell her how he felt about her, maybe she'd give him more of a chance. She seemed to like him.

Snooper came up and stared at him.

"You want to go home, Snoop?"

The dog seemed to nod and trotted off in the direction of the truck.

Buck knew where Stephanie hung out sometimes. Maybe he would swing by Shirley's Bar and see if she was there. If she wasn't, Buck would keep checking until he found her. She hadn't been answering her phone the last few days. She hadn't showed up at work either.

Buck had decided he would say something to her, maybe even ask her to marry him. Maybe that's what she wanted. He knew he could be persuasive. It helped to be six-four and weigh in at over 270 pounds. Working at the pet food factory lifting hundred-pound bags kept him in great shape.

"I'll tell her, Snooper."

The small dog stood up next to him in the car seat, his tiny paws up on the dashboard, and turned to stare at him with his eyes, dark brown as a coffee bean. He often struck him as smarter than most people Buck knew, and certainly more willing to listen.

"I'll say—Stephanie, you be my woman and marry me, or I'll kill myself. You think that'll do it?" Buck chuckled.

Snooper wagged her tail at the sound of Buck's voice.

"It's a plan."

"Hey, baby."

Stephanie's heart sank when she heard Jack's voice on the other end of the line. She had hoped it might be Buck. That was why she had answered the phone. But now that she had answered the phone, she knew she needed to talk to him. Otherwise he would get mad and come over to teach her a lesson.

"Hi." She tried to keep her voice calm.

"It was good to see you the other night. You've put on a little weight, but it looks good on you."

"You looked good too," she said. She knew he needed to hear that. He was a handsome man and loved to hear her tell him how fine he looked. Women loved to look at him.

"Thanks, baby. What're you doing?"

She hated that he always called her baby. Why couldn't he ever use her real name? "Not much. Haven't gone to work since you stopped by."

"Why not?" he asked, sounding surprised.

"Because I look like shit."

"Why do you say that, baby?"

She couldn't help it. She was getting mad. "You saw to that. A big black eye, bruises all over my face. Can't go to work looking like that. All your fault."

"I don't know what you're talking about. I thought you looked fine when I left."

She hated it when he did that, denied what he had done. "What're you talking about, Jack? You beat me up good. Choked me. Why do you pretend that nothing happened? Do you think I made it up?"

Silence. Not a good sign. Then he said, "You know I would never do anything to hurt you. I love you too much for that. But I'll tell you one thing, if I ever did beat you up, you wouldn't be alive to talk about it."

She recognized the signs. His voice was getting lower. He was getting mad—she could hear it. It was time to get off the phone before she said something to really provoke him. "I gotta go, Jack."

"Why's that? Is that boyfriend coming over? I wouldn't count on him, baby. You never know what might happen."

3

MEG knew he would be back in to talk to her in a moment or two. She determined not to cry. She was a big girl, and that never helped anything. Except sometimes with Mom. Mom hated to see her cry, but Meg did reserve it as a weapon of last choice. She heard Mr. Turner's footsteps echoing down the hallway. Like clock ticks, they were even and steady and would not turn back.

Mr. Turner was her fifth-grade teacher. She had never had a man teacher before and had really been looking forward to it. There was something more adult about being taught by a man. He had dark, spiky hair, long legs, and hairy eyebrows. Some of the girls thought he was cute. Meg thought he looked like a smooth-talking devil.

She hadn't at first. She had liked him like everyone else. But then he started picking on her. He didn't want her to read in class when she was done with the assignments. All her other teachers had always let her read in class. It was the only way she had gotten through school so far. Otherwise it would have been too dull and boring waiting for everyone else to finish. But the first time she had tried to read, Mr. Turner had taken her book away and asked her to clean the blackboards for him.

When she tried again, he had taken her out into the hallway and talked to her. "This is a school classroom where we do schoolwork. If you are finished with the work I have given you, then I want you to raise your hand, and I will give you some more work to do. Or better yet, check over your work. If you are doing it so fast, there are probably mistakes you should correct."

Meg hadn't taken either of his suggestions. Instead, she had done the only thing left to do. She had slowed down. She was doing the work as slow as she could, and it was killing her. Boredom weighed her down like a ton of bricks. That's what had gotten her in to trouble this time. She had been so bored that her eyelids had closed, her head had dropped onto her desk, and she had fallen asleep. Mr. Turner had woken her up by tapping the top of her head with a pencil. She had jumped and given a little shriek. The whole class had laughed. He had asked her to stay after class when it was time for recess.

She sat at her desk and stared down at a small mole on her arm. It was about the size of a ladybug. Wouldn't it be cool if it started to move around her arm? She could have a pet mole. She laughed at her own joke just as Mr. Turner walked in the door.

"Can you let me in on your joke?"

Meg freaked at the thought of trying to explain to him the way her mind worked and the pun she had created. "Just remembering something from TV last night."

"Meg, what are we going to do with you?" he asked.

Her mind, at times like these, could be her own worst enemy. It was still trying to make jokes, and was coming up with answers like: Give me an A and send me home for the day, A crown might be a nice choice of headwear, Let me be the teacher and you can be the student. She had to bite the inside of her mouth so that she wouldn't start laughing again.

"Meg, can you answer me?"

These were trick questions. It never did any good to try to answer them. She knew that Mr. Turner had an answer all ready and was dying to tell her what he had thought up to do with her. So she just shook her head.

"You didn't finish your work on time, and you fell asleep during class. I had such high hopes for you when you started this class, Meg, but I can see your bad attitude is getting in your way. Since you are so sleepy, I think we should let you have a little nap so you can stay awake for the remainder of the day. So while the rest of the class is outside playing, I want you to put your head down on your desk and close your eyes."

Meg looked at him in disbelief. She needed to get out and play with everyone else. This meant she would be trapped at her desk for the next half hour, and she knew she wouldn't be able to sleep. "Mr. Turner, I will try—"

"No, Meg. It's too late. I must show you that I am the boss in this classroom. You don't know what's best for you. I do. Please put your head down." He stared at her, his eyes boring into her like laser beams.

She put her head down. At least she didn't have to look at him. But she could feel him standing there, watching her. He did have complete power over her. He could make her do anything he wanted her to do. She hated him. She hated school. She hated life. She felt the tears backing up behind her eyelids. She bit the insides of her mouth again, trying to hold them back. She would not let him see her cry. She knew that he would like that.

Claire had been given the call from the Bank of Alma to handle. Janet Stone, the bank manager, told her that it appeared

that someone was forging signatures on one of their customer's checks. The account had been overdrawn, which had
called it to their attention.

"This woman, Mrs. Tabor, is in her eighties and not in
good health. I'm worried that someone is taking advantage of
her. The checks were written out to cash and then cashed at
our branch down in Alma. Mrs. Tabor has her account with
us here in Pepin. As far as I know, she never does business
down at that branch. They wouldn't know her there. When
we examined the two checks against the signature we have on
file, it was not a match."

"How much money are we talking?"

"Each time the check was written for one hundred dollars. Not a lot, but for Mrs. Tabor it probably equals groceries
for the month."

"I'll check into it." Claire got Mrs. Tabor's telephone number and called the woman. After talking to the older woman
for a few minutes on the phone, Claire decided it might be
better to handle this case in person. The woman seemed con-
fused and distraught. She had told Mrs. Tabor that she would
drive over to see her. It was about seven-thirty in the evening,
but Mrs. Tabor assured her that she didn't go to bed until
nine at the earliest.

One night every two weeks, Claire worked late. She
traded with another deputy, Billy Peterson, who was taking a
night class. It suited her fine. Gave her a chance to fill out all
those never-ending forms that she meant to stay on top of,
but often didn't. And she hoped it helped her be more like one
of the guys at work. It was hard to be one of the guys when
you were the only woman and the only investigator.

Being investigator meant that she mainly worked a regular day shift. The sheriff had decided they needed someone to
oversee their higher-profile cases. There weren't many—
mostly burglaries and once in a while a little fraud.

Mrs. Tabor's case sounded like it might involve some
fraud. Claire drove out into the country, down a dirt road that

wound through the coulees. Finally she came to Tabor Lane. County roads, if they were dead ends, were named after the last farm on them. Claire drove another half mile, until the road ended in a farmyard. It looked rather deserted, but there was a light on over the front door. No dog barking, which was a relief. She liked dogs, but feared them in people's yards. Just last month Ted Schultz, another deputy, had been badly chomped by a dog.

Claire got out of her car and went to the house. She knocked on the door loudly and waited half a minute before pounding again. Then the door popped open, and a very small, severely bent-over old woman stood in the doorway.

"I heard you, it just takes me some time to get out of my chair and all."

"Sorry. I just wanted to make sure."

"Making sure is good. My goodness, you really are a deputy?" Mrs. Tabor looked at Claire's uniform.

"Yes, ma'am, I am."

"What a good idea to have women working as police. I always think they are more sensible."

"Sometimes."

"Would you follow me into the living room? It's warmest in there."

"I won't take up much of your time, Mrs. Tabor."

"Time is all I have right now, so don't worry about that."

They sat down—Mrs. Tabor in a small stuffed armchair that had an old flowered chintz fabric that looked out of place in the farmhouse, Claire across from her on a plain brown couch.

"I stopped by the bank and picked up copies of the checks."

"There was more than one of them?"

"Yes, there were two. Each made out for one hundred dollars. Supposedly signed by you. Let me show them to you. You might recognize the handwriting. Does anyone else write out your checks?"

"Oh, my, no. I would never allow that. I'm on a very tight budget."

Claire brought out the checks, and Mrs. Tabor pulled a magnifying glass out from under the cushion of the chair. She stared at them, turned them over, and looked at them again. "That's not my signature. My handwriting's gotten awful bad. It's hard to read, but the bank knows it's mine."

The signature on the checks was easy to read: it was more printing than writing.

"Who has access to your checkbook, Mrs. Tabor?"

"Well, there's my daughter, and then there's Lily. She comes in three times a week to straighten up around here and makes me a nice meal or two."

"Do you think either of them might have done this?"

"Not my daughter. She doesn't need the money. Her husband's got a good job."

"What about Lily?"

"I can't think she would do this. It's not like her at all. She makes the best meatloaf. She's coming tomorrow. Should I ask her?"

"Do you feel safe doing that?"

There was a pause that made Claire feel uncomfortable. "She has a bit of a temper," Mrs. Tabor said.

"Let me come back and talk to her. It might be better if the questions came from me."

"I'm sure she didn't do it."

Claire nodded. "You're probably right, but it's good to check."

They agreed that she would come the next day and speak with Lily. Mrs. Tabor showed her to the door and turned the porch light on to light her way to her car. She stood in the doorway until Claire drove off and waved as she turned onto the road. Claire left with a strong sense of a lonely woman, dependent on others.

When Claire got back to the sheriff's office, she searched out Scott Lund. He lived in Pepin, which was one town down from Fort St. Antoine, and was in the know about a lot that went on in that area. She wanted to ask him about Stephanie Klaus.

She found him sitting next to the coffee machine, watching the coffee filter down.

"Not quite enough for a cup yet?" she asked him.

"I try not to do that. Take that first cup. I think it weakens the whole pot."

"Thoughtful of you."

"My middle name."

"Hey, do you know a woman named Stephanie Klaus?"

Scott tapped his empty coffee cup on the counter as he thought for a moment. "Don't think so. Where's she live?"

"She lives in Fort St. Antoine on the highway. I think she's lived there a year or so."

"No, doesn't ring a bell. Why do you ask?"

"She got badly beat up the other day, I think. Remember when I was asking about any news of a domestic? Well, I think she might have been the one who called me. I saw her at the post office, and she did not look good."

"Stephanie Klaus. Doesn't sound familiar. I'll ask around." He pushed his hair back. "Man, I hate domestics. They are the worst. One time I went out to a place. The woman had called. I go out. The kids are crying, the husband's drunk as a skunk, holding a baseball bat. I try to get him, and the next thing I know the woman has a hold of me and is biting my arm. Biting me. I got out of there and called for backup, and we hauled them both in. I had teeth marks in my arm for a month or two."

"Did you need a rabies shot?" Claire asked.

Scott sputtered a laugh. "Naw. She wasn't a bad woman. Just completely goofed up. She wouldn't prosecute her husband, but I did get an assault on her. She had to go and see a counselor. Hope it did her some good."

"You never know."

"Did you talk to her?"

"Stephanie?"

He nodded.

She thought of the dark bruises flowering on Stephanie's cheeks. "Not yet. I'm going to try to stop by and see her this week."

Claire had wanted to do some checking on the computer to see if Stephanie Klaus had ever reported getting beat up. It might give her a handle when she went to talk to the woman. When she went into the computer she found nothing in the county and nothing in the state. But she knew that didn't mean squat. She didn't know the exact figure, but most domestic abuse cases went unreported.

Claire leaned back in her chair. If her middle-of-the-night call had come from Stephanie Klaus, Claire had to take it as a good sign. It meant Stephanie was reaching out. Maybe she was ready to turn this guy in. Claire decided to go and talk to her the next day.

Buck felt something cold splash on his feet. His head hurt, but he knew he needed to wake up. Something was very wrong.

Water was on his legs. He opened his eyes. Where the hell was he? He could tell that he was in his car, but where was the water coming from? Where was the dog?

His head wouldn't work. But he hadn't had that much to drink at Shirley's. He remembered walking outside. Then it all went black. What had happened? He tried to get out of the car, but found he was tied in. There was something around his neck. He couldn't pull free.

Then it came to him. He was in the lake. His car was floating half in and half out of the water, but it was filling fast. Water was up to the seat, and it was pouring in through the top of all the windows, gushing on top of him, drenching him. Ice water.

He struggled with whatever was fastened around his

neck, tying him to the car. He couldn't get it loose. His hands were freezing. The water was up to his chin. The car was tilting back.

He strained his head up, trying to keep it above the water.

The whole car was pulling him down. He thrashed around trying to get free and let out a roar. Who had done this to him?

He tried to breathe, but the water came in his mouth, and he was choking on it. He couldn't hold his breath. He reached his hands up as high as they could get, but the water covered everything.

Cold beyond thinking, he took in his first lungful of water. It was his last.

4

Afew minutes after midnight, the end of her shift, Claire climbed into her car to go home. She fumbled with the key and made several attempts to get the cold car started before it roared to life. By this time the inside of her windshield was fogging up. Claire held her breath, swiped at the patch in front of her eyes with a paper napkin, and then turned the defrost up to high. A small hole of clarity appeared in front of her, enough visibility to begin her long drive home.

As she was leaving the building, Scott had told her that the temperature was only three above zero and dropping. Another brittle cold night.

When she was nearly to Highway 35, Claire heard Lorraine issue a call over the radio that a car had been reported going through the ice at Scottie's Point on Lake Pepin. Claire answered her and said she'd respond to the call, as it was on her way home.

Every year this happened. Claire couldn't believe how stupid men were when it came to driving out on the ice. The siren's call, it must be, all that clear expanse of smooth frozen lake, just waiting to be driven on. Add a little alcohol to their system, and they didn't even try to resist the impulse. But it didn't happen too often on Lake Pepin. Maybe the men had more respect for the huge body of water, were a little more aware of the dangers of a lake thirty-two miles long and in some parts two miles wide.

Since she'd worked for the sheriff's department, the only incident had been last year when a couple of snowmobilers had gone through the ice, at the spot where the Rush River fed into the lake, and the warmer, flowing water had kept the ice thin. The snowmobiles were lost, but no one had gotten hurt.

By midwinter the ice on the lake would be frozen so solid that it could be used as a road to drive across the lake to the Minnesota side. People who commuted there daily saved a good twenty minutes cutting across the lake, but now it was still too early to venture out on the ice.

Scottie's Point. Claire knew where that was, out past Shirley's Bar. She was becoming familiar with that lowlife place; she had had to haul a guy out of there twice when she was working the late shift. She accelerated past sixty. She was about five miles away from the scene.

As she turned off the highway and drove past the bar, she saw two vehicles down at the point. She drove down the dirt road that led to a natural bay in the river, pulled up next to a pickup truck, turned her brights on aimed at the lake, and stepped out of her car.

The car was quite visible in the white stream of her headlights, half in, half out of the dark water, held up by a jagged rim of ice. It looked like an old Chevy Nova.

Two men were standing side by side, staring out at the lake. They turned their heads toward her at the same time, then back to the dark hole. The back end of the car stuck out of the ice, the trunk and a portion of the window above water.

One of the men said, "I was out back of Shirley's and heard the ice crack, and then I saw the car drop in."

"Is there anyone in there?"

"Not sure," one of the men said.

"Probably," the other chimed in.

"Somebody had to have driven it out there," the first man reflected. "How else would it get there?"

She leaned back into her car and radioed the department. "We need an ambulance here. And I need some help. Contact the fire department."

"Ambulance is already on its way," Lorraine told her.

"Thanks, Lorraine."

"Whose car is it? Any idea?" Claire asked the two men.

"Not sure. Might be that one guy's, works out at the W.A.G. factory. Forget his name. You know who I mean, Stewy?"

Stewy shook his head. "Don't think I know that guy."

"Probably not. He's only been in to Shirl's a few times. You might not have been there."

"How long ago did it happen?" she asked them.

"Dunno," they both said in unison.

Claire took a tentative step out onto the ice. It had been cold the last few nights; the ice would hold her. She pulled down her hat and turned up the collar of her coat. A wind blew off the lake. She hoped no one was still in the vehicle. Whoever it was had already been in the water far too long to survive—although she had heard weird tales of what submersion in cold water could do. A few years back, a young boy was pulled out of a lake up by Fargo after fifteen minutes under, and he survived. The cold had slowed his metabolism down so far that he didn't have much damage. Lost a few toes. But they said such a recovery was more apt to happen in the young.

What idiot would drive out there?

She heard a car pull in and turned to see Scott jumping out of his car. "I wasn't far behind you. Decided to join the party."

"Thanks. I think I better try to get out there. They think

there might be someone in the car. You got a rope in your car?"

"Yeah. What're you thinking of doing?"

"Let's tie it around me, and I'll inch out there. If you hear the ice crack, or if I scream, you can pull me in."

"I'll go out on the ice," Scott offered.

"Forget it. What do you weigh?"

Scott laughed. "A little more than you."

"Might make a difference."

Scott pulled a heavy rope out of the trunk of his car. He tied it around Claire's body, up high under her arms.

Claire held her arms up in the air as he finished and said, "I don't want to go in the water."

"I won't let you go in."

"Good."

Scott patted her shoulder and looked her over. "You've done this before?" he asked.

"No."

"Okay, this is what you want to do. First get down on your hands and knees. Take this with you." Scott handed her a standard flashlight. She stuffed it in the pocket of her parka. "Go slow and steady. Stop dead if you hear anything."

Claire felt hugely undignified, crawling out on the ice on her hands and knees. But no one was laughing. She slid her hands forward slowly, trying to keep the weight evenly distributed on all four points of contact with the ice. She could feel the cold coming up through the thin leather gloves she was wearing. She needed to start carrying her heavy choppers in the car.

The car was about thirty yards off shore. When Claire got about ten yards away from the hole, she heard Scott shout behind her. She turned her head and lifted up her ear flaps to hear what he was saying.

"Get down, now. All the way down. Then inch forward."

She understood why she needed to prostrate herself on the ice, but she felt very vulnerable doing so; the ice gave way, she would be in the water headfirst. But the ice seemed quite stable beneath her. She slid herself forward with her feet, pushing off with her toes.

When she got within five yards of the car, she could see something in the interior, some large shape. She pushed herself a little closer and, for the first time, felt the ice shudder beneath her. It had to have weakened where the car had gone through.

She heard a siren coming down the road and guessed it was the fire department. Thank God. Those guys knew what to do; ice rescue was one of their specialties.

Claire pulled out the flashlight and shone it into the car. She stared and saw what she had feared to see: a white hand reaching up to the ceiling of the car, floating in cold water, and a white oval underneath it that might be a face staring up at the air.

She couldn't resist. She pushed herself forward another inch. It was an inch too much. The ice cracked beneath her, and the suck of the coldest water she had ever felt pulled her down.

She held her breath and felt the water engulf her face and the top of her body. She thrashed around and tried to grab onto something with her hands, but there was nothing there but cold water. Her bottom half was still on the ice. She tried to stroke with her arms, pushing down in the water, to raise her head up out of it.

At the instant when she didn't think she could hold her breath for a second longer, she felt a jerk around her waist. Then, like a fish, she was pulled back up onto the ice, and like that same creature, she turned over on her back and tried to catch her breath, mouth open, stars in her eyes.

Stephanie walked into the bar and saw that Lee was in her favorite booth. She waved and walked over.

"What happened to you?" Lee asked, looking at her face.

"Oh, nothing. Just fell down. Slippery ice."

"Man, you must have fell right on your face. Yow."

"I'm pretty clumsy." Stephanie looked around the bar. "Have you seen Buck?"

"He was in earlier, but then he left. Haven't seen him since. You supposed to meet him?"

Then Stephanie saw the little dog sitting at the end of the bar. "Nothing definite. What's Snooper doing here?"

"Huh. Now that's odd. Buck takes him everyplace. Wonder if he just forgot him. Maybe that means he'll be back.

"He'd never leave Snooper."

Stephanie walked over and picked up the dog, who immediately washed her face with its soft tongue. She had never had a dog in her life, and they usually scared her, but Snooper was different. He seemed to understand what you said to him as he stared up with his deep brown eyes.

"Where's Buck?" she asked him, and he stopped licking when he heard the name and looked at her.

"Buck?" she repeated.

The dog squirmed in her arms. When she set him down, he ran to the door of the bar, so she followed him. He scratched at the door, and she let him out, but once out in the parking lot, he ran around and then peed on a rock at the edge of the parking lot.

She said, "Buck," again, and he sat down and stared at her.

Stephanie reached down and picked the little dog up again, rocking him in her arms. "I don't have a good feeling."

The pager went off just as he was standing on top of his barn, trying to do a pirouette. Clay Burnes slapped his hand down hard on the bedside table, hoping to find the pager before it sang again. On his second thwap, he found it, as his wife turned over and groaned.

"Don't wake up," he mumbled to her. "It's for me."

She pulled the covers over her head, knowing what would come next.

Clay launched himself out of bed to make the call. He went into his office and hit the button set to dial the sheriff's department.

"Yeah, Burnes here."

He was told he was the third EMT to call in, and when he heard where the ambulance was going, he told Lorraine he would meet it at the scene. He only lived a mile from the lake.

Clay wanted a cup of coffee bad, but knew he had no time to do anything but throw on clothes and go. He tried to be out the door within minutes of receiving a call. His best time was under a minute. He looked at his watch: 12:15. He had been asleep for less than two hours.

He pulled on the jeans and sweatshirt that he kept at the ready in a pile next to his bed. He patted the top of his wife's head. She didn't even stir.

In his kitchen, he grabbed a Coke out of the fridge. Car keys in hand, he went out the back door and climbed into his Ford pickup.

He was on the road before he thought about peeing. Damn. It would have to wait. All the dispatcher had told him was the place and that a car had gone through the ice, possibility of someone inside.

There wasn't a vehicle on the road as he wended his way down off the bluff. Good thing he could drive these roads in his sleep.

As he came down Highway 35, he could see the lights of the fire engine and various sheriff's department cars lined up at the lakeshore. He was glad to see that the fire chief was there already. They were the ones with the ice rescue training; they had done a course out on the Chippewa River a year ago. EMTs were always told to stay on shore, to stay out of the burning house. They were never to put their lives in danger, because then they wouldn't be there to aid the survivors.

The ambulance pulled in right behind him. Ladders were

being laid down out onto the ice as Clay walked down to the shore. Deputy Steve Murphy was talking to the fire chief, and Clay heard him say that Watkins was the incident commander. The woman deputy must have been first on the scene. She was walking around with a blanket wrapped around her shoulders and he wondered if she had gone into the water. She wasn't afraid to go out on the line, you had to give her that.

Clay liked her. She took charge, which some people had a hard time doing. He had worked with her on a car accident, and she had kept things running very smoothly. His wife had wanted to know all about the new woman deputy when he came home after the accident. He had ended up describing her as "intense, but calm."

"Anyone out there?" he asked as he walked up to Watkins.

"Yeah, but I think he's a goner." She looked at her watch. "I've been here five minutes already. God knows how long he was under before I got here. We'll just have to wait and see when the fire chief can get him out."

Clay stood and looked out at the back of the car sticking out of the water. Suddenly he felt like ice water had been poured down his body. "Whose car is that?" he shouted.

"I don't know," Watkins said.

"I think I know."

She looked at him, waiting.

"It's my nephew's. His name is Buck Owens." Clay hated the words coming out of his mouth.

"I'm so sorry." Claire took a step toward him, but then stopped and pulled her blanket tighter around herself.

Clay looked out at the car sticking out of the ice. "I don't get it. He would never do something so dumb as driving out on the ice. What am I going to tell my sister? That was her only kid. She loved him like he was a saint. He wasn't that bright, but he was a hell of a nice kid."

✦

Dr. Lord drove up in his rust-fringed old Volvo station wagon. He had a tweed cap pulled over his bald head and a down vest worn over a flannel shirt. Stepping out of his car, he appeared to be moving rather slowly. Maybe his arthritis was acting up again. He didn't mention it often, but Claire knew it affected his hands sometimes while he was working.

She was surprised how glad she was to see him. As if he were a dear old friend at a party full of people she didn't know, she ran up to him and said, "Thanks for coming down at this time of night."

"Indeed," he said, smiling. Then he stared at Claire, wrapped in the white flannel blanket that the ambulance crew had given her to dry off with. "This the new style?" he asked.

"I went for a swim."

He shook his head, looking her up and down. "I'd advise against it this late in the year."

"Advice taken, but it's a little late," Claire said as she brought Dr. Lord over to where the body was laid out by the firemen. "I'm glad you could come out. I wanted you to see the body before it was moved again."

"We oldsters don't sleep that well. A little break in the middle of the night is not unusual. What happened?"

Claire walked him up to the covered body of Buck Owens as they talked. She explained what she knew. "Car went part of the way under the ice. His head was tied to the headrest, so he was under water. He was probably dead before I even arrived on the scene. But only minutes. They did try to resuscitate him, but it did no good."

Claire reached down and pulled the sheet back. Dr. Lord slowly lowered himself down on his knees beside the wet and sprawling body and put on a pair of latex gloves. Deftly he checked over the body, looking into the eyes, the mouth, the ears, taking the temperature by putting a thermometer far into Buck's mouth, even though he told her it wouldn't be very accurate.

"I'm sure the water brought his temperature down fast. I know it did mine."

"This kind of ice water can lower the temperature quickly. I have some charts back at the office that will tell me how quickly."

"He's carrying a little extra weight. Would have kept him warm a little longer."

"Yes. He looks like a strong young guy," Dr. Lord commented.

Claire filled him in on what she knew of the man. "Buck Owens. Twenty-five years old."

"This is where he was tied?" Dr. Lord pointed to the ligature marks circling Buck's thick neck.

"Yes—as I mentioned, when I found him, he was tied to the headrest in his car with a red rag. The rag had been wrapped several times around his neck. So when the car went into the lake, he couldn't get out of it."

"I'd say he put up one hell of a fight to get free, pardon my French. Somebody pretty big must have done this."

"Or he was taken completely by surprise."

"Perhaps."

"Do you think he was dead when he went in the lake?"

Dr. Lord gently moved the head back and forth, staring at the marks on the neck. Then he reached up for a hand from Claire. She pulled him up, and he patted her hand in thanks. "Claire, Claire, a little patience."

"We're about to take some photos."

"Yes, let's do that and then move this body out of here. I have seen enough. His extremities are beginning to freeze. None of us need to be working out in this frigid weather."

"Cold as a morgue."

"A comment like that from you?" He smiled at her. "What time might I expect to see you tomorrow?"

"When would be convenient?"

"Late afternoon would be perfect. Come a little early, and you can watch me at work." He waved and walked away. The proper gentleman, Claire thought, no matter how dirty his hands might be.

The first time she had come to watch him do an autopsy, he had been a little put out, never having had to perform for the sheriff's office before. But now she felt that he looked forward to her company. He was the only medical examiner she had known who seemed to still regard the body he was dissecting as a human being. He treated them gently, almost reverently. But then, unlike the medical examiners in the Twin Cities, he maybe only got one or two bodies a month to examine.

The tow truck was pulling the car out of the water behind them. Claire turned and watched. The truck started right on the edge of the frozen lake and chugged slowly down the dirt road, pulling the car out of the lake like an icebreaker.

"Just take it into Durand for tonight," Claire had told the tow company. The crime bureau could send someone out in the morning. And she had a present for the lab. She felt it in her pocket: the glasses that had been on Buck's face, sealed into a plastic bag. Maybe they would get lucky and pull a print from something in the car or even from the glasses.

Scott came walking up. "I went and checked out the bar. There were a couple of drunks helping the owner close. The owner said that Buck had been in there tonight. Didn't stay long. Owner thought some guy he didn't know had come in, but couldn't remember much about him except that he was big. Said he thought it was funny when Buck left his dog."

"Dog?"

"Yeah, I guess Buck owned some kind of little dog, and they always let him bring it into the bar. When Buck left, he didn't take the dog with him."

"Strange. He must have thought he was going to return. Where is the dog now?"

"The bartender said his girlfriend took it home."

"Oh, and who is that?"

"All he knew about her was that her first name was

Stephanie. He said they had come into the bar together a few times."

Claire stopped when she heard the name Stephanie Klaus? What might this mean? "Did he describe her?"

Scott looked back over his notes. "Didn't say much. Not a very talkative guy for a bartender. Said she was a young blond."

Being blond didn't narrow the field very much in Wisconsin. "So Stephanie and Buck came in the bar together?"

"He didn't think so. The way he remembered it was that Buck came in and left, and then Stephanie showed up. Said she seemed a little upset over finding out that the dog had been left there all alone. Said she just took the dog and left herself. This was right when they got the news about the car going in the lake."

"This bartender sounds like one sharp guy."

"Just doing his job."

There was an easy way of finding out if this Stephanie was the Stephanie with the bruises. Go over to her house and see if she had the dog.

5

RICH woke up and turned over and looked at the glowing dial of the clock next to the bed. Three-twenty. Claire was almost three hours late getting home from work. Not good—it could only mean trouble. Usually the night shifts were very quiet, and she often got to leave early. She had surprised him on more than one occasion as he slept in the recliner chair in front of the TV.

He flopped over and tried to go back to sleep. He counted sheep, then switched to pheasants, then turned on his back and counted his breaths. When he got to two hundred, he decided to get up.

He could always call the station. They would be able to tell him where she was, what was going on, but he would feel like a worrywart if he did that. Claire had warned him about what her life was like. She had told him that it was a lot more normal now that she was working for a sheriff's department, but she said that her hours were erratic and her time was not always her own.

"We might plan to do something, and I'll end up having to

cancel. Or you'll want to go to a movie, and I'll have to catch up on some work. Or you'll want to tell me about your day, and then I'll need to tell you about mine, and it won't always be fun listening."

Rich felt that in the beginning Claire had almost tried to scare him off. He knew a lot of that had been about her own fears—learning to trust someone again, learning that not everyone you loved would die on you—but some of it had been about her own indecision about being in a full-blown relationship.

He was beyond ready to be with someone. He had waited a long time to find a woman like Claire, almost giving up hope that he ever would. It scared him that he felt as if he would do almost anything to keep her.

Turning on the light next to the bed, he watched the shadows gather in the corners of the room. Slowly, trying to make no noise, he swung his legs out of bed. He had left an old flannel bathrobe at Claire's, and he pulled it on and tied it around his waist. He walked softly out of the room and down the hallway, not wanting to wake up Meg. He had found her to be a light sleeper.

Down in the kitchen, he filled the teakettle with water and then pulled open a drawer next to the stove. Postum with a little warm milk. That should send him back to sleep. He lifted the top off the cookie jar. Two Oreos left in the bottom. Perfect. He made his hot drink and brought his snack out to the full-season porch, where the TV sat perched on top of an orange crate.

Claire had splurged this fall and bought a satellite dish, which he had installed. Satellite was the only way they could get decent TV reception down in the river valley. Since then he had become slightly addicted to the Weather Channel.

He sat down in the recliner and set his hot drink on the window ledge next to him, the two cookies piled up next to his cup.

His mom would meet Claire in a few days. He wondered

how that would go. His mother had not cared for his first wife; she called her a little tart, in no nice sense of the word. He hadn't felt like explaining to his mother that he liked the slightly overt sense of sexuality that Tina had displayed. And unfortunately his mother had been right in the end; maybe Tina had been a little bit too much of a hot tamale for him.

Claire, too, could be quite sexual, but it was more controlled. And this sense of restraint in her was all the more appealing to Rich. When he touched her and got her warmed up, he felt as if he was seeing a part of her that few men had ever seen. He felt very lucky.

But he wondered if his mother would pick up on that. She had a kind of radar for a willing woman.

The other thing he worried about was how strong both of the women in his life were. They were independent, opinionated, mouthy women. They might really hit it off, or they might not. Thanksgiving would tell.

Rich sipped his drink, ate one of the cookies, and then turned on the Weather Channel. Blue-and-pink pulses of light moved across the United States. A perky blond woman said that skies would clear overnight in Florida. Hurricane season was well over. He had enjoyed watching those storms move across the Caribbean, so far away.

He wondered what the weather would bring them. It was dropping down to under ten degrees tonight. He hoped that Claire wasn't out in the cold. Then he thought about how he would have to warm her up when she got home. He watched the clouds drift through the satellite skies. He set his cup down and closed his eyes as the woman with the soft voice told him how cold the northern tier of the United States would be. Below zero. Nasty cold. Icy.

Snooper tucked her head into Stephanie's thigh and whimpered as they pulled out of the parking lot. The silky fur of the small dog reminded Stephanie of a lamb she had petted once on her grandfather's farm. A small comfort.

"I know it's cold. I'll get you home soon," Stephanie prom ised the tightly curled-up dog.

A few minutes ago two guys had come into the bar, saying that a car had gone through the ice down the road a ways. Didn't look good, they said. Stephanie called Buck, but all she got was his answering machine. She decided to head home and check out the accident on the way.

As she drove down Highway 35, she heard a siren, and then a cop car went sailing by her. She was glad she hadn't had anything to drink in case she was stopped. She didn't want to have to explain anything, certainly not why she was interested in the accident. As she rounded a curve in the road, she could see down to the lake and the tangle of cars and trucks that were lined up by the point.

She pulled off the road and watched what was going on. Not wanting to be in the way, she pulled off the track she had turned onto so that any vehicle could get by her.

She knew it was Buck who had gone through the ice.

She knew it before she saw the large, familiar body stretched out on the ground, before she saw that it was his old Chevy Nova they were trying to pull out of the lake. Before she saw how everyone moved around the body, not really paying it much attention, she had known he was dead.

She had always known she would never get to stay with Buck. He was a gentle soul whom she didn't deserve. He had treated her like she was worth something, and she had tried to push him away. Now she was sorry that she hadn't pushed harder. Because of her, Buck was dead.

Jack had killed Buck. She didn't know how he had done it; she hated to think about that. She knew it as well as she knew her own name, as well as she knew that someday he would kill her too.

She had to freeze herself. She had learned how to do that

many years ago. In order to get through the beatings, the fear, the relentless waiting, she had learned how to turn her mind off and make her body move forward. That part of her that cared about people, she needed to disconnect it from the rest of her mind. It had never done her any good anyhow.

Stephanie reversed out of her parking spot and turned back onto the highway. Get home, she thought.

When she pulled up into the driveway, she saw that the porch light was off. Maybe it had burned out. She tried to tell herself that as she got out of the car and walked up to the house, Snooper following at her side. Then the little dog stopped and relieved himself on some bushes.

"Come on, Snooper," she called, needing to hear the sound of her voice in the still air.

The dog wagged his fluffy tail and carefully stepped over the rocks in the driveway. Stephanie walked up the steps to her house and tried her door. It was locked—a good sign. She inserted her key and slowly opened the door. Nothing. She reached inside and turned on the outside light and the light in the kitchen. Empty. Still nothing. She stepped into the house and let Snooper come in behind her.

Before she could do anything else, she needed to check out the house. She walked through the kitchen and into the living room. Everything as she had left it. The rug she was working on was sitting in the corner behind the couch where she had put it, red and green for Christmas. She had thought it might be nice under the Christmas tree. It all seemed like an odd dream—the holidays, Christmas, presents for Buck, good cheer, ho-ho-ho—what had she been thinking? She was halfway done with the rug, and now she might never finish it.

Then she checked the bathroom, pulling the shower curtain to one side to see into the bathtub. Finally her bedroom. Nothing looked disturbed.

She went back into the kitchen, sat down at the table, and stared out into the night. She needed to go to bed. She would go to work in the morning. She would work until payday on

Wednesday and then leave on Thursday, which was Thanksgiving. She would tell no one anything about where she was going—not her mom, not anyone. This time she would completely vanish.

Snooper was sitting in the middle of the kitchen, his nose pointing up at the sink.

"What do you want, Snooper? You need a drink of water?"

He stood up and wagged his tail, happy at her ability to communicate with him.

She reached up and got down a bowl and filled it with water.

"You're going with me. I need a buddy."

It was three in the morning. If she was going to be in any shape for tomorrow, she'd better try and get a few hours of sleep. No one would be in very good shape at the factory once they heard about Buck. He had been well liked. She thought of the locket he had given her. She kept it in her jewelry box. She would take that with her. But she would take little else. Only what she could pack in the car.

She walked down the hallway to her bedroom. Sitting on the edge of her bed, she started to shake. Don't, she told herself. Don't think. Just go to sleep.

She stood up and pulled back the covers, ready to crawl into bed in her clothes, when she saw the red. Something red was all over her sheets.

She dropped the sheets and screamed.

Then she saw what it was.

Rags. Red rags. From her weaving. He had come into her house, taken a handful of the rag strips that she used for her rug, and put them in her bed just to show her what he could do.

She knew what he could do.

He would kill her, but not tonight.

And maybe if she planned well and went farther than he would even dream of her going, she could get away before he got her.

✦

He watched the lights go on throughout the house, leaving a trail of her movements. He wondered if she would stay in the house when she found what he had left her. If she went any-place, he would follow her. He would not let her get away this time. It had taken him all too long to track her down.

A roaring filled his ears. Anger at her bounced around in-side his belly. He hated the thought that that stupid fucking punk had touched her body. It would never happen again. No other man would ever touch her.

He was the only one who had any right to her.

He had been her first lover, and he would be her last. He would see to that.

A woman was supposed to be faithful to her man.

They were born for each other. He had told her that for-ever.

His eyes focused on the bedroom. He could see so clearly in the dark. He had left the shade partly drawn up in her bed-room so he could watch her. He loved watching her when she didn't know he was doing it.

She turned on the light in the room, looked around, and left.

His eyes could see everything. They could pierce her skin and go into her mind. He always knew what she was thinking.

He was working on controlling his anger, not letting it control him. It made him very powerful, his anger, and if he could use it the way he wanted to, he would be able to do any-thing.

The key to this control was steady breathing and holding in. He did not always give in to his sex drive when he felt it. He often let it build up inside him just to feel the steam of it swirl around.

But still, he needed other women. He could not hold it back forever. That was not his responsibility.

He watched her come back into the bedroom. When she pulled back the covers, he saw her face. The shine of holy fear. She was worshiping him again.

He would not go to her tonight. She would want him, but he would hold back. It would bring him more power.

He would have her again soon enough

And then he would have her forever.

She was his.

When Claire walked in the door at four in the morning, she heard the gentle drone of the TV and found Rich slumped over in the recliner. His face was tilted to the side, and his mouth was slightly open, letting a soft whistle escape as he breathed. He didn't look all that comfortable.

She hoped he hadn't been there all night. She felt enormous relief to see him in her house.

How comforting to come home to a sleeping man.

She was beyond tired, hungry, cold, thirsty, and sad. She wasn't sure how she would face the day that would begin all too soon. This case needed to be attended to immediately. Her mind began to whir at what she would have to check into in a few hours when she went to work: Stephanie, autopsy, the checks for Mrs. Tabor, the car, Buck Owens's parents.

Claire stood in the middle of the room and put her hands to her temple. Let it go. You need to sleep. It will all happen soon. She shook herself and then looked again at her sleeping lover.

After turning off the TV, she walked quietly over to where he sat in the chair and knelt in front of him. She reached out her arms and laid them on either side of his waist, and then she bent over and put her head in his lap. He was warm from sleep. She felt him stir, and then she felt his hands smooth back her hair.

6

DAMP, thick clouds hung low over the lake, obscuring the bluffline across the water. From the window in her bedroom, Claire looked out. Clouds had settled into the crooks of the coulees on the far side of the lake, resembling lost sheep. The inside of Claire's head felt like how the sky looked—muffled and woolly—but at least she was up and moving around.

She had slept until nine and eaten a large breakfast, knowing she would need the calories to get through the day. Rich, bless him, had already gotten Meg off to school without waking her. He had made her breakfast and told her not to worry about the dishes. If he was trying to make himself indispensable, she thought, he was doing a darn good job of it.

As she came down the stairs from her room, she saw he had his down jacket on and was ready to go out the door.

"Arctic out. It's not even above zero yet," he told her.

She groaned at the thought of the cold day ahead. The brutal cold made everything harder to do.

"What are you up to today?" she asked.

"Going over my books."

"Counting your pennies?"

"That's about it. Nothing as exciting as what you will be doing—looking at another man's naked body."

"Don't forget, I'm also having pie with an older gentleman."

"And I thought a cop's life was tough. I'm going to have to meet this Dr. Lord sometime."

They kissed an easy kiss, and she waved him out the door.

She called in to the department before she left the house to tell them she was on her way, and Julie warned her that the sheriff wanted to see her as soon as she got in. This came as no surprise. Claire had called him last night from the scene when she realized that the car going through the ice was not an accident, that they might be dealing with a murder. He had listened, and when she told him that the car was out of the water and they were ready to load the body into the ambulance, he said he'd be right down. He wanted to see the scene himself.

Claire stopped by Stephanie Klaus's house before she drove on to work, but there was no sign of anyone. No car, no dog. She had knocked on the door of the small house just to see if a dog would bark, but she had heard nothing. Could another Stephanie have been seeing Buck Owens? One way or another, she needed to find out today.

Half an hour later, when she walked into Sheriff Talbert's office, he seemed in a decent mood. Even though he was in some ways a figurehead, with Chief Deputy Swanson doing the hands-on in the department, he made his presence known. He had hired her, and they had always gotten along.

"Mighty cold last night," he commented, then added, "Glad I could make the party."

"Always glad to have you," she told him.

He lifted his mighty eyebrows and then let them fall. It was a good sign. "Steve's already talked to me. I know you're on top of it. I'm not complaining. Don't get snarly with me, Claire."

"I'll try not to."

A smile crept onto his face. "Wish I would have been there a little earlier. I would have liked to see you go for a little swim."

"Scott fished me out pretty darn quick."

"He said it looked like someone had tied this guy up and then drove him into the lake."

"Yes, I'm going over to get the results of the autopsy in a few hours, but I think it will just confirm what we saw."

"What the hell's going on? Any ideas?"

"Yes, sir, actually I am formulating something."

"Care to share?"

Claire hesitated only for a moment, knowing that Sheriff Talbert kept a closed mouth as well as anyone. "Well, I could be all wrong, but there's a woman in Fort St. Antoine who appeared to have been beaten up pretty badly last week."

"I remember you asking around about that."

"Right. From what I learned last night, there's a chance she might be Buck Owens's girlfriend."

Sheriff leaned his head in his big hands and squeezed. "Shit. Not a burning mattress type-a-deal?"

"It's a possibility. I don't want to rule it out."

"You'll know soon." It should have been a question, but the sheriff didn't let it come out as one.

"I plan on finding out the girlfriend's name and talking with her sometime today."

"Keep me posted."

Before she even went back to her desk, Claire tried to run Scott to ground. Julie said he had been in and out. Bob said he was in the computer room. She finally found him coming out of the john.

"How did his parents take the news?"

Scott leaned against the wall in the hallway and winced, remembering. "I hate that part of being a deputy."

"No one likes it."

"I like giving out tickets."

Claire was glad someone did, "What was their reaction?"

"Let's see. The mom sat right down on the floor and cried, and the old guy cracked his knuckles and swore."

Claire felt her heart break a little for this couple she hadn't even met. "Did they say anything about a girlfriend?"

"They said they knew he was seeing someone, but they had only met her once. They didn't remember her name."

"Did they tell you anything we didn't know?"

Scott shrugged and then repeated, "They said everybody loved Buck. No one would ever want to hurt him."

The map of the world was always pulled down near the front of the class, and Meg found her eyes drawn to it. She would imagine herself in a plane flying all over the world. She thought about all the places she would travel to when she got older, after college. Maybe her mom could come with her to some of the places: they could eat Chinese food in China, buy a kangaroo for Rich in Australia, shop for lovely lace in Switzerland. But the places she really wanted to visit were those little islands in the middle of nowhere. The most middle-of-nowhere islands were the ones in the Pacific Ocean, like Wake or Johnston or Midway. She wondered how big they were, and if you could walk across them in a day. She imagined that some of them, in a really bad storm, like one of those tsunami waves, maybe would get completely washed over with water.

"Meg, do you see something by the blackboard?"

"I'm just thinking, Mr. Turner."

"Working on your math problems?"

"Yes, sir."

"Good," he said.

She bent her head over her math paper. She was behind again. The time was almost up, and she had ten problems to do. She raced along and managed to get five more done before Mr. Turner began to collect the papers. But with five problems not finished, she couldn't expect to get an A, probably not even a B. What was happening to her this year?

At least another school day was over. Everyone was getting ready for the bell to ring. She didn't even feel like taking her homework home. She knew she had a bad attitude, but she wasn't getting anywhere with Mr. Turner. She didn't seem to be able to please him. She grabbed her history book, her math book, and her worksheets and headed for the door.

"Meg?" Mr. Turner's voice stopped her.

"Yes."

"Is your mother going to be able to make conferences?"

Meg felt her stomach drop. Conferences were the week after Thanksgiving. What would he tell her mother? "I think so."

"I know she works during the day. I could schedule her to come in toward the end of the day."

"You should probably talk to her."

"Yes, I'll do that." Even the way he said that made her stomach turn. Maybe that's why his name was Mr. Turner.

Mrs. Tabor was waiting for dinner. What was taking Lily so long?

Lily knew she liked to eat a big meal at lunchtime, right at noon. That's when she had always eaten her big meal. When her husband was alive, she often baked biscuits, some kind of meat, potatoes, and a vegetable. He had never said much, but from the way he wolfed down the food, she knew it was appreciated. Once or twice a week, she'd try to make a pie. Herman had loved his pie. His favorite was raspberry. For a few weeks in the summer, she would go out and pick raspberries and make him pies.

She didn't know what Lily did some days. Nothing seemed to get done. Then other days, she would whirl around and clean the kitchen and make a fine meal.

"Lily?" Mrs. Tabor thought of getting out of her chair to see if she could help.

"Don't fuss, Mrs. Tabor, it's almost ready."

Mrs. Tabor put her watch under her magnifying glass. Nearly one o'clock. No wonder she wanted her dinner.

Then Lily came in, carrying a tray. "There you are."

A pile of yellow—must be corn. A mound of brown—probably meatloaf. Then a blob of creamy white. Her favorite, mashed potatoes. Her dentures had been bothering her lately, so she was glad to eat mushy food.

A knock at the door.

"Who could that be?" Lily asked.

Mrs. Tabor remembered that the deputy lady was coming. She didn't say anything, but started eating her food while Lily went to answer the door.

Then Lily ushered in the lady, who introduced herself again as Deputy Watkins.

Mrs. Tabor said hello and continued eating her food. She didn't want to appear to be part of the questioning.

"Lily, the bank called us. It appears that someone has been forging some checks of Mrs. Tabor's. Do you know anything about this?"

"Why would you even ask me? I just come in and make her a meal every few days. If anything shady is going on, it's that daughter of hers. She only stops by to take something from her mother. Isn't that right, Mrs. Tabor?"

Mrs. Tabor made a noise in her throat. She loved her daughter, but Lily was with her more often. She needed to watch her step.

"Could I ask you to write out Mrs. Tabor's name on a piece of paper for me?"

"No, of course you can't. Think I don't know better than that? I watch the TV. I know my own rights. I don't need to sign nothing."

"This is a criminal offense. I can take you down to the sheriff's office, and we can continue our conversation there."

"Let me see those two checks."

"I didn't say anything about two checks," Deputy Watkins said.

"Well, the reason I said that number is that I helped Mrs. Tabor with two checks last week. Her eyesight is getting so bad. Remember, Mrs. Tabor?"

It was hard always to remember everything. Lily helped her with so much. What would she do without her? "I think I do," Mrs. Tabor said.

The deputy showed her the two checks.

"Sure enough. Those are the ones."

"Well, the bank is overdrawn as a result of these two checks."

"Her social security check should go in today, so they will be covered," Lily said.

Mrs. Tabor wondered how she knew that. It went directly into her bank account. Had she told Lily that?

Deputy Watkins squatted down alongside Mrs. Tabor and touched her arm. "Is that what happened? Did Lily help you write those two checks? And then take them to the bank to cash them for you?"

"Oh, yes. I'm sure it's fine, then. If Lily says so." Mrs. Tabor could feel the deputy staring down at her. She didn't dare look up and face those eyes.

Deputy Watkins voice was calm, not sounding like she suspected anything was amiss. "All right. I'm glad we got this cleared up. You call me if you ever need anything. Looks like a good lunch."

"Lily's a real fine cook. She takes good care of me."

The deputy patted her on the shoulder, and Lily showed her out the door. Mrs. Tabor waited for Lily to come back into the living room, but she must have stayed in the kitchen. Her potatoes were cold, but she finished them.

She felt awful sleepy. She hoped Lily wouldn't be mad at her today. She could be so mean sometimes. She never knew what to expect from her.

Buck Owens body lay gutted in front of Claire, chest cut wide, head opened up, and body parts removed. She could see that the bags they had placed over his hands were removed and the fingernails clipped down to the quick. Somehow that bothered her more than the chest torn stem to stern.

She had missed most of the autopsy, but had come in time to have Dr. Lord show her the damage to his neck. And his pièce de résistance—water in the lungs. "Lake Pepin water," he had told her. "I'm guessing it's Lake Pepin water. I'll send it down to the lab. I'll have to match it. Drive out to the lake later today."

"Don't go in yourself," Claire warned him.

"Did you ever get warm last night?"

Claire ignored his jab and asked the next logical question. "So he was alive when he went into the water. Can you tell if he was conscious?"

"No conclusive way to determine that, but I would guess, unfortunately, that he was."

"How so?"

"By the damage done to his neck. I think he struggled fiercely to get loose, and I think that probably happened when he went into the water."

"Yes, I see." Claire sat up on a high stool he had given her while Dr. Lord walked around the body, poking and picking and prodding at it. His last task was to draw blood directly from the heart for alcohol determination, toxicology, and blood typing.

"What do you think happened to him?" Claire asked.

"He got into his car after a beer or two. This is a guess, but given what I know, I think he strapped himself in with his seat belt. He leaned his head back, and someone grabbed him around the neck and tied him from behind to the headrest in his car. Didn't you say the firemen had to cut him loose?"

Claire nodded.

"Then I think he passed out for a bit. His eyes show signs of strangulation. The perpetrator might have choked him first before he tied him up. Then the car was driven into the lake, and he drowned."

"I'm trying to figure out how they got the car into the lake."

"Car an automatic?" Dr. Lord asked.

"Yes, it is."

"Head it in the right direction, give it enough gas, and it will keep going until the ice cracks under its weight."

"Did the strip of cloth fit the marks on his neck?" Claire asked.

"Yes. I think it was triple-strength around his neck. When it got wet, it really cut into his neck, but he couldn't break it."

"What do you think it is?"

Dr. Lord brought out the bag with a red strip in it. He held it out for Claire to look at. "I'm not sure. Some kind of rag, but why would it be cut like that?"

"A rag strip." She stared at it. Long thin red rag. She remembered where she had seen them before. "I should have thought of this sooner. I think I know what it is."

7

Stephanie couldn't believe she was at work, checking over dog food as it went into big paper bags. There were moments when her blood would turn to ice in her veins and her feet would feel frozen to the factory floor. She would wonder if she could even move if she had to run for her life.

She hadn't been able to leave Snooper at home—the thought of anything happening to him made her start to shake—so she had brought him with her. She checked on him a few minutes ago, to make sure he was okay sitting in the car with a big polar fleece comforter, a bowl of food, and plenty of water. She had parked so the car would be in full sun all day long. She had checked on him twice in the morning and then taken him for a long walk at lunch. He seemed quite content and very happy to see her. He had a very sunny personality.

Nearly as sunny as Buck's had been. She knew it was stupid, but somehow she felt as if something of Buck lived on in Snooper, some of his kindness. She needed to hold on to that.

The foreman of the factory had made an announcement

about Buck's death the first thing at the start of the shift. After telling everyone what had happened, he had asked for a moment of silence. Stephanie had felt all her fear and tiredness waiting to drop her to the floor, but she remained standing.

Afterward, he had walked over and said, "I'm sorry, Steph. I know you guys had something going."

She had nodded, accepting his condolences silently. She didn't want to start crying at work.

Throughout the day, people had stopped by her station, mainly the women, some she hardly knew, just to say a little something. Most of them were awkward and all they might say was, "Too bad," "So sorry," but she knew it was heartfelt. Buck had always had a smile for everyone. Even though she knew they were offering her sympathy because of the way they had felt for Buck, she still appreciated it.

The one good thing about being at work was that she was safe here. Maybe she should sign on for extra shifts. Two more days, and she would be gone. She just needed to get her two-week paycheck. It would make a big difference on how far she could go.

She was even thinking of Hawaii. She had never been there, didn't even know anyone who had ever been there, but she didn't think she would ever be found there. She would get a little carry case so Snooper could fly in the plane with her.

It was hard to do her work when she was so tired. They kept track of how many bags each checker did an hour, and she knew her average productivity was not going to be what it usually was. But she stayed at it, steady as she could be, trying to keep awake on the line. At least nothing dangerous would happen to her if she fell asleep. Some people could get really hurt if they weren't careful.

Thinking of Hawaii kept her going. Palm trees—she had never seen a palm tree. Drinking right out of a coconut. Maybe she'd even learn how to hula dance. She and Snooper could go for long walks on the beach.

She'd legally change her name. Stephanie Klaus—she had never liked her name. Maybe Lorna Lake; that had a nice sound to it. She could be a totally different person. A woman who never took shit from any man. Maybe she would find someone to love her. Maybe she would get married again. Kids were certainly still a possibility.

She got giddy when she thought of what her life could be. But when she thought about leaving her house, getting away from him, she started to sweat. She knew he would stay away from her for a while, but then he would come after her. She did not want to think what he would do if he found her.

"Claire?" Bridget said when she heard her sister's voice. She hated to call her at work, but she needed to talk to her. "Or should I call you deputy?"

"Call me madame."

"Madame it is."

"What can I do for you?"

"You busy?" Bridget didn't know why she asked. She could tell by Claire's voice, the professional remove in it, that she was.

"Sort of."

"I'll be quick. Is there any chance Rachel and I can come for Thanksgiving?"

A pause—she could hear papers rustling. "I thought you were going to Chuck's folks."

It wasn't a good sign that Claire hadn't immediately been thrilled with the prospect of two more for Thanksgiving. "Well, Chuck and his dad decided they wanted to go deer hunting."

"Oh, deer hunting. He's going to miss his baby's first Thanksgiving?"

"You don't need to rub it in. I'm not happy about this decision."

"No, I suppose not. Of course you can join us. Rich's mother is coming too."

This explained the reticence. "Oh, I didn't know."

"Yeah, Rich just asked if she could come."

"You haven't met her before, have you?"

"No."

"Is there any way I can help?" Bridget grimaced. She felt she needed to offer, but she wasn't known for her cooking.

"Yes," Claire said. "Could you bring a nice bottle of white wine, and can you be responsible for the relish tray?"

"Yes, absolutely. I can do the relish tray. I would love to do that. I'll make it look really nice. Don't give it another thought."

"Thanks, Bridge. It'll be nice to have you with us. I know Meg will be ecstatic when she hears that Rachel will be there. How is the little cutie?"

Bridget looked over at the small sleeping form, curled among pillows on the couch. "She's fine. She doesn't seem to like to sleep in her crib. She wants to be with me wherever I am."

"That's sweet."

"She'll get over it, won't she?"

"Oh, in about ten years. Then she won't hardly want to be in the same room with you."

When they hung up, Bridget walked over and knelt down by her baby. Rachel was pursing her lips in her sleep. Hungry again? Bridget hoped not for another hour or so. Her breasts ached with their intermittent fullness and then the constant feedings. Rachel didn't seem to take that much at a time and so was hungry an hour or two after she had fed. Bridget had made the big mistake of figuring out how many hours a day she was breast-feeding. When she came up with four and a half, she started crying.

Bridget felt like she was living in a dream world; never really awake and certainly never really asleep. She slept with one ear out for the slightest whimper from Rachel.

She was petrified that Rachel was going to die. She knew it made no sense. She knew that it was a common feeling among new mothers. But none of this knowledge helped her deal with the raw anguish and absolute panic she felt whenever she wasn't sitting, watching or holding her baby.

She had dreams that she had forgotten about Rachel, not fed her for days, completely forgotten she had even had a baby, until she found her lying on the floor in her bedroom. The dreams would wrench her from sleep, and she would have to go and see that Rachel was all right.

At Thanksgiving, she would try to talk to Claire about this. Maybe she would know some tricks to help her calm down.

Bridget was mad at Chuck for going hunting, but in a way she would be glad to be rid of him for a few days. He loved Rachel and held her and even changed her diapers, but he didn't like how much attention Bridget gave her. "Let her be," he would say. "She can cry for a few moments. She'll be okay."

Rachel was almost a month old, gaining weight, waggling her feet in the air, and looking at everything. She was a healthy, happy baby. But sometimes Bridget did wish she were ten years old. Or eighteen, going out the door to live in her own apartment.

It wasn't that Bridget didn't want to enjoy all the years of Rachel's growing up, it was that she could hardly wait for the time to come when she would know that she had done her job, raised her darling daughter to adulthood. She hated feeling so responsible for another person.

Two people sat hunched up over the long wooden bar and didn't even turn around to look as she walked in the door. The bartender was smoking a cigarette near the one window at the far end of the bar.

With an incredible view of the lake, Claire couldn't understand why they didn't have any windows overlooking it. Instead there were two small windows at the front of the bar looking out into the parking lot.

The place smelled like a wet ashtray—beer and cigarettes—what a mixture. In a neon sign, the Budweiser beer
horse team was galloping over the cash register.

"What can I do for you?" the bartender asked, walking
over to where Claire stood by the bar.

Claire would have guessed his age to be mid-fifties. It was
hard to be sure as drinking and smoking had obviously taken
their toll. The skin around his eyes sagged so much that it was
hard to see his pupils. His thinning hair was greased across
his balding head.

He looked pointedly at her uniform, then asked, "You in
here about what happened at the lake last night?"

"Yes, were you here?"

"I wasn't, but Norm filled me in."

Claire took down the name of the bartender who had
been working the previous night. "Do you know Buck Owens,
the man who went through the ice?"

"He died, didn't he?"

"Yes, he died. Did you know him?"

"Not really. I knew who he was to see him and all."

"Did you ever see him in here with a woman? I've been
told her first name was Stephanie."

"Yeah, I know her. She's not bad looking. Comes in now
and again. Doesn't even drink too much. I think she and Buck
worked together or something."

"Do you know where she lived or what her last name
was?"

"I think she lived in Fort St. Antoine. And I remember her
name. Someone teased her about it. Klaus, like Santa Klaus.
But I think she pronounced it differently."

So it was Stephanie, her neighbor. Felt odd to have it be
someone she knew. This never happened to her when she
worked in Minneapolis. "How did she and Buck get along?"

"They weren't a big item. Seemed almost more like
friends. They'd meet here sometimes. Never caused a com-
motion, if that's what you're asking."

"Did Buck ever cause any trouble?"

"Buck?" The bartender laughed. "You gotta be kidding. Couldn't have been a nicer kid. If you ask me, almost too nice. Helped anybody out. Even when he got drunk, he stayed nice. Some guys do that. They get kinda sweet and slobbery. Know what I mean?"

"Yes, I do. My husband got sentimental if he had a drink." Claire was surprised to hear herself say that. She didn't talk about Steve very often, but that behavior reminded her of him.

"Sorry to hear that Buck was killed. I'm also hearing it might not have been an accident. Is that true?"

"We're checking into that."

"Take it to mean it's true, otherwise you'd deny it." He looked Claire over. "I've heard about you—the woman deputy. Guys talk about you in here. You're even prettier than they say."

Claire nodded her head at the compliment. Before she turned to walk out the door, she couldn't resist saying, "Smarter too. Thanks for the info."

8

STEPHANIE didn't care if she didn't finish the rug. She had to weave. She needed something to keep her hands busy, and weaving soothed her like nothing else. The only other thing that worked for her was drinking, and she didn't want to start doing that. She had to keep her wits about her. That was something her mother would say. Her mother had lived with a man who was very similar to Jack, Stephanie could now see. Very similar.

Snooper sat next to her on the couch and watched her as she moved the shuttle back and forth. His head moved as her hand did, and she could have sworn that he was trying to learn how she did it. He was such a smart dog.

She hadn't paid much attention to him when Buck was still alive and had always been rather astonished at the degree of Buck's attachment to the dog, but now she felt like she understood it better. He seemed like a remarkable animal to her: devoted to his master, whoever that might be, and attentive in a way that she had never experienced before. She felt utter love coming off the dog, but sometimes he gave her the willies. Like he was reading her thoughts.

At night, in her double bed, he would curl up on the pillow next to her head. He would fall asleep before she did, but in the morning when she woke, his eyes would be fastened on her face.

"What do you think, Snooper?" she asked.

The little dog wagged its tail, pounding it against the couch cushions.

"I should make you a little rug. Something for you to lie on that would be your very own."

He wagged again and this time gave a small yelp.

She laughed. "You like that idea."

She was more than half done with the rug, and it was turning out nicer than she had hoped. A green stripe and then a red stripe. She was making it two and a half feet wide and the same length—a square to fit under a small tree.

She remembered the first Christmas after she had fallen in love with Jack. She had thought he was everything. They had opened presents early Christmas morning. He had given her a pair of earrings, boasting that even though they were zirconium they still cost him fifty bucks, and she had given him a CD that had the song "I've Had the Time of My Life" on it. It was their song. She had also knit him a scarf, which he said was too precious to wear. She thought he didn't like the way it looked on him but was afraid to tell her. He had gotten through that phase fast.

She also remembered that they had made love later on that day. He had made her put on her earrings, and then he had touched her all over in places she had never been touched before. She had the thought that she wasn't sure if she was in love with him, but she knew that her body was in love with his. She had been only fifteen.

Her hands moved on their own over the rug, and her thoughts could go where they wanted to. But she had to quit thinking about Jack. He wasn't who he once had been. He hadn't been that man for many years. She had put up with him for far too long.

Then there was a knock on the door. She froze. Only one more day, and she would be gone. Please don't let it be Jack. She couldn't let him see the dog. He might hurt it—he was mean to animals. She scooped up Snooper and put him in a crate that she had gotten from work, then she gave him a treat and hid him in the back of her closet, telling him to be quiet.

Whoever it was continued to bang on the door. She smoothed her hair down and peeked out the small window at the top of the door. A woman. Then she recognized the woman. It was the deputy woman, Claire.

For an instant Stephanie fantasized about telling her everything, pleading with her to help, but then she remembered what had happened last time. She had sworn never again. She would take care of herself. The police never listened.

She opened the door.

Claire tucked the Polaroid of the red rag in her purse before she left her house. She had stopped home before she dropped in on Stephanie, feeling that this was an instance when her uniform would not serve her well. She had changed into a sweatshirt and jeans. Let Stephanie see that she was just another woman, that she might understand what she had gone through—maybe that way she would open up and talk, telling Claire what had happened to Buck.

As Claire drove over to Stephanie's house, she felt very odd to be stopping over at a neighbor's to see if she had killed someone. When she had worked in Minneapolis, she had never interrogated anyone she had known personally. She felt very uncomfortable and wondered if she should have come with Scott or Billy. Made it more official.

When Stephanie opened the door, she flung it wide as if

she had nothing to hide. "Oh, hi," she said as if she had been expecting someone else.

"I need to talk to you."

Stephanie didn't say anything, but continued to stare at her. Claire stared back, surprised by how small the woman was. Claire put her height at under five-foot-three and wouldn't have guessed she weighed more than a hundred and ten pounds. The bruises on her face had faded until they looked like a smear of makeup in the wrong spot.

"Just a few questions," Claire added.

"That sounds ominous."

Stephanie's use of the word surprised Claire. It stopped her for a moment. What did she know of this woman? What had she presupposed? She needed to start over again.

"I don't mean it to sound that way. I guess I just thought it was time we talked. I'm Claire Watkins. I work for the sheriff's department."

"I know who you are. Come on in." Stephanie's shoulders dropped, and she stepped out of the way, allowing Claire to come into her house.

Claire followed her into the living room. A 1960s-style sofa with a teak frame and what looked like the original fabric sat up against the wall.

"I like the sofa," Claire said before she sat down on it.

"Salvation Army. Thirty bucks."

"These sixties pieces are getting trendy again."

Stephanie ran her hand over the fabric and said, "Reminded me of one we had when I was a kid."

Then Claire looked at the work set on the tiled coffee table. Stephanie was weaving a green-and-red rag rug. The red strips looked like a match to the one that had been found tied around Buck's neck.

"I love your rugs," Claire said and then felt disingenuous saying it. But she did love Stephanie's rugs. How to be both a neighbor and a cop at the same time? "I do a little quilting. Is weaving hard?"

Stephanie smiled for the first time. She looked Claire full in the face. "That isn't why you came here."

Claire said honestly, "I wish it was. It's about Buck."

Stephanie's head dropped and she nodded. "I thought so."

"Do you have the dog?"

"Oh, the dog." Stephanie stood up and ran out of the room, returning a minute later with a small, fluffy dog under her arm. "I forgot about him. I had put him in his crate."

"What kind of dog is he?" Claire asked, looking at the tawny powder puff with deep brown eyes.

"A Pomeranian."

"What's his name?"

"Snooper."

"Kind of a silly name."

Stephanie looked at Claire and nodded. "Yes, I've been thinking of changing it. Maybe just adding on to it. Gentleman. Gentleman Snooper. It would suit him better. He has more manners than most men I meet."

Claire decided she better get down to it and ask Stephanie some serious questions. As she was reaching into her purse, Stephanie stood up.

"I could make some coffee?"

"No, that won't be necessary."

"I don't have anything to eat in the house." Stephanie looked toward the kitchen.

"Really. I need to ask a few things about Buck. Sit down."

Stephanie did as she was told.

Claire held out the Polaroid of the red rag. It was taken against a white sheet and stood out well. "Do you recognize this?"

"What kind of question is that?" Stephanie pointed at the rug she was weaving. "A trick question? Of course I do. It looks like one of my strips of red cloth. Why?"

"No trick, Stephanie. Calm down. It was found in Buck's car. When we dragged it out of the lake." Claire had decided she would tell her no more than that.

Stephanie squinted her face. "His car? Let me think. I know what might have happened. I think I brought my weaving over to his house one night, and I bet that piece fell out of my bag."

Not a bad explanation. Claire went on. "Do you know what happened to Buck? How he died?"

"Just what everyone knows. His car fell through the ice. I assume he drowned."

"Did you see him that night?"

Stephanie answered quickly—maybe too quickly. "No. We had talked of meeting at the bar, but when I got there, only Snooper was still there. Buck was already gone. I was surprised."

"Was he meeting anyone else there?"

Hesitation. "No, not that I know of. He didn't say anything to me."

"What was your relationship with Buck?"

Stephanie's eyes filled with tears, but she blinked them back. "I guess you might have called us girlfriend and boyfriend. I don't know. We were more friends as far as I was concerned."

"Stephanie, it looks like someone tied Buck into his car and then drove it out onto the ice. It looks like he was murdered."

Stephanie didn't react. She stroked the dog who was leaning into her lap. "I wondered."

"You don't seem surprised?"

"Because Buck would never have gone out on that ice. He knew better. He wasn't dumb like that. He knew that lake better than anyone I know."

"Do you know anyone who might have wanted to hurt him?"

Stephanie snorted. "Buck? No way. He might have annoyed some people, but he was too nice for his own good."

"Did you have anything to do with what happened to Buck?"

Stephanie's eyes widened. It wasn't much, but Claire had been watching for it. "No. I don't think so. Not that I know of."

"How could you not know?"

"Maybe somebody at work liked me. Maybe someone had a grudge against Buck. I don't know."

Claire tried a different tack. "Who beat you last week? Was it Buck?"

"You've got to be kidding. Buck literally wouldn't hurt a flea."

"Then who did it?"

"My own clumsiness. I admit it looked bad, but it all happened when I fell down my front stairs. They had gotten icy in the night."

"Stephanie, I think you need to tell me what really happened."

Stephanie looked at Claire and then said a little more loudly, "Why are you asking all these questions? Do you think Buck beat me up, so I killed him?"

Claire sat still.

"You do, don't you? Why the hell would I do that? Why would I kill the nicest man I've ever known? Can you answer me that?"

Claire watched her.

Stephanie picked up Snooper and held the dog up to her face, burying her face in the dog's fur. Her shoulders shook as she started to cry. Then she lowered the dog into her lap and looked at Claire with tears flowing down her face. "Why would I take his dog home with me?"

"A good question."

Stephanie gave a squeak of a laugh. "Maybe that's why I killed him—so that I could get the dog."

"Don't worry." As soon as the words were out of his mouth, Rich wished he could clap them back.

Claire reacted the way he thought she might. She stopped

pacing in the middle of his kitchen and snapped at him, "Don't tell me to not worry. I hate it when someone does that to me."

"Fine."

"Fine?" She burst out laughing and sat down next to him. "Thanks for that. I'm being a jerk, aren't I?"

"I hadn't noticed. Let's see if I've got this right. You went over to a neighbor woman's house who you suspect has been assaulted recently and whose rag rugs you like, and you asked her if she had killed her boyfriend, and she said no, and now you feel shitty for having accused her."

"She has his dog, for God's sake."

"I'm on your side. I'm on her side."

"I think she liked this guy. I don't think she was in love with him, but I think she thought it might happen. From everything I know about him, he was a nice man. And now he's dead. But I do think she knows something she's not telling me. I think she might have an idea who did it."

Rich watched her work through all this.

"But what if I'm wrong? What if he beat her, and she killed him?"

"Don't you think you will figure that out—that something will give it away?"

"God, I hope so. But someone did beat her up. She tried to tell me that she slipped on the ice, but you don't land on your face and have bruises around your eyes if you fall. Only another person pounding you leaves marks like that. How am I going to get her to talk to me about it?"

"Try again."

"You're right. Persist, as my father would say."

Rich decided to change the subject. "You ready for us all tomorrow?"

"I think so. It will feel weird to me not to be working on this case over the holiday, but nothing will change, and it will give the crime lab more time to analyze what they've got. The house is pretty clean. Is your mother fastidious?"

"She keeps her house clean, but not always neat. Anyway, don't worry about what she'll think."

"That's easy for you to say. Both my parents are gone, so you will never be faced with this."

Rich could tell she was spoiling for a fight. He didn't want to go there. "What would you like me to say?"

Claire thought about it for a moment. "That your mother will love me."

He took her hand and held it to reassure her. "I can't promise that, but I know she will like you."

"That everything will go off like clockwork."

He lifted her hand to his lips and kissed it gently. "Better than that, we will all have a good time."

"That I will find who killed Buck and I will find them fast, before anything else happens. I'm worried about Stephanie."

"Does she seem scared?"

Claire thought back to Stephanie. "Numb would be a better word. When I told her that we thought Buck had been killed, she didn't seem surprised. More resigned. Like she'd been waiting to hear that."

Rich thought of his pheasant chicks. "When one of my chicks is being pecked at, after a while, they give up."

Claire gave him an appraising look. Then she stood up, walked over to his coat closet, and took out a scarf. She wrapped the ends around both of her hands and then walked behind him and wrapped it around his neck. "I want to do an experiment. Try to get away from me."

9

"OU'RE not going to believe it, but we got a latent off of Owens's glasses," Clark Denforth, the head forensic specialist at the state crime lab, told Claire over the phone at work. He was an excitable guy, and he was excited.

"After he was underwater?"

"Yes, and it wasn't his own print. Checked that right away. Someone who, shall we say, perspires freely. For whatever reason, he had very greasy hands. We got a great, clear print off the lens. And best yet, it was a tented arch."

Claire knew enough about fingerprints to know that this was one of the rare ones. "That will certainly help in identification."

"You got anyone for us to look at?"

She paused and thought of Stephanie. "Not yet, but hopefully soon. Wish you could tell sex from a print."

"I call with great news, and all you can do is complain."

Claire walked down the hallway to confer with Chief Deputy Sheriff Stewart Swanson, known as Stewy to everyone. He ran the department while the sheriff did the public business. Not that the sheriff didn't step in, but they seemed to have worked the division of labor out between them and were a good team. Stewy was riding this case with her.

She found him at his desk, looking out the window into the sky. "We're gonna get some weather." He continued to stare out the window as if he were hoping to catch the first snowflake that fell from the sky in his gaze.

"Do you feel it in the air?"

"No, heard it on the radio."

"We could use some snow."

"What've you got?" he asked her.

She told him.

"Great," he said, "but we have no suspect."

"We have one, but I don't think she did it."

"Who?"

"The girlfriend."

"Not a bad choice."

"She's quite a small woman. I don't think she could have wrapped that tie around his neck and secured him to the headrest."

"Adrenaline."

"Not even with adrenaline. I tried it on a friend, and I couldn't keep the guy from getting out of the seat and breaking away from me. She's a lot smaller and a lot weaker than me. I just don't think she could have done it."

"I trust you on this, Watkins."

He was calling her Watkins. This meant it was very serious. She knew he wanted this case solved pronto. The Owenses were well thought of in the county, and winter was a long and hard season even without a murder case dragging everyone down. "Thank you, sir." If he could be formal, so could she. "I told her to come down to the station so we could fingerprint her. She agreed to do that. Friday, she's coming in."

"She said she'd come down?"

"Yes, without hesitation." Claire continued. "The problem

is that her fingerprints legitimately might be all over his car and even on his glasses. They were seeing each other. She's got the best excuse in the world. She told me that the rag was in his car because she dropped it there. So anyone could have used it to tie him up."

"You don't think she killed him."

"I have no extrasensory perception, but she didn't act that way to me. She acted like she was thinking about something else."

"Like what?"

"Like she was thinking about how scared she was of who had killed him."

"She wouldn't tell you?"

"I couldn't get it out of her."

"Why didn't you bring her down right then?"

"I didn't think it was the way to play it. She's not going anyplace. She's got the dog. She's got a good job. She's established. Let me try to get through to her. I won't let her slip away. I drive by her house at least twice a day. I'll keep a good eye on her."

"I'd say haul her down if it weren't Thanksgiving."

When Claire got back to her desk, there was a note telling her to call Dr. Lord. She dialed a strange number and found she had reached him at home. His wife answered and passed the phone to him.

"You're not working today?"

"My patients are too busy shopping for turkey to come in and see me, which suits me just fine. My wife needed my assistance in making the cranberry sauce. We make quite a bit and put it up for the winter."

"Organized."

"I had a thought." He paused and then went on. "It's a strange thought, but I decided I should mention it to you."

"I'm all ears."

"Yes, of course you are, my dear. But your hair covers them nicely."

Claire didn't honor that with a response.

"What I was thinking was that there is a chance that Buck killed himself."

Claire sat down in her rolling chair and it rolled a little. She pulled herself back up to her desk and wrote down, *Suicide?* "You think so?"

"Not really. I mean I don't think he did, but when I went over how it happened, I realized he could have tied himself to the headrest, drove himself out onto the lake, knowing he wouldn't have been able to get the ties off in time to save himself from drowning."

"Yuck."

"A possibility."

"Well, if Virginia Woolf could load her pockets up with stones and walk into the Thames, I suppose Buck could tie himself to his car. I'm going out to talk to his parents shortly, and I'll try to find out more about his state of mind."

An hour later, Claire drove down the driveway of a large farm on the bluff. The view of the lake up the valley was spectacular. She pulled over for a moment and looked down at the ice-covered lake glistening in the subdued sunlight. It did look as if some weather was moving in.

The farmhouse was set back from the bluff, so it didn't have as much of a view, but probably got hit with less of the wind.

Claire's knock brought a woman in her late fifties to the door. She guessed it was Mrs. Owens. She was tall and heavy with a pile of white hair on her head. Her eyes were very blue in her pale face.

Without saying anything to Claire, the woman turned her head and shouted into the house, "Herb, it's the police. Come and talk to this lady."

"May I come in?" Claire asked.

"Oh, lord, yes. Where are my manners? Please come in. We're sitting in the living room. The TV is on, but we're not really watching."

When they walked into the room, her husband turned the sound down on the TV, but the contestants on a game show still tried to answer the silent questions. Mr. Owens was taller than his wife but lean as a whip. His lips were thin and drawn in his weathered face. He nodded at her, then pointed at the TV.

"It's noise," he said, "but sometimes noise is good."

"Let me say how sorry I am for your son's death."

Mrs. Owens face cracked open, her mouth twisting, and she sat down on the couch and bowed her head.

"Thank you," Mr. Owens reached out and shook her hand. "He was a good son to us. The best."

"Do you have other children?"

Mr. Owens shook his head. "No, I'm afraid not."

"Did he live with you?"

"No, he moved out a few years ago. He thought it was time. We miss him, but he stops by nearly every day. He did. He moved into Bay City to be closer to work."

Claire asked them for names of friends. Then she asked, "How'd Buck been feeling lately?"

Mr. Owens looked puzzled.

"Had he seemed in good spirits?"

"Well, you know that kid loved this time of year. He's a hockey player, and he loves to get out onto the lake and skate. He's always loved winter. Such a big kid, he never got cold. Did he, Mother?"

Mrs. Owens lifted her head and shook it. "No, it was hard to keep a coat on him. He moved too much. He got too warm all the time."

"How old was he?"

This time Mrs. Owens answered. Claire had noticed that women kept track of such things. "He would turn twenty-five in January. He was born the first of the year. Our New Year's baby. Remember, Herb?"

"I sure do. We drank champagne before and after he was born. That's when women still drank when they had babies. I know they don't do that now. But Mother was sure happy to have that baby."

"Had anything been bothering Buck lately? Had he talked to you about anything? Anything new going on in his life?"

"Well, he was seeing this new girl," Mrs. Owens said. "We only met her once. He brought her up here for a barbecue when Herb's brother and kids were here. I didn't get to talk to her much. She seemed kinda quiet, but nice enough. Wouldn't you say, Herb? Nice enough."

"Yeah, she seemed fine. Buck liked her. That's the main thing. We wanted him to be happy." The older man's voice broke, and he looked at the TV, blinking rapidly.

"Were they getting along?" Claire continued with her questions even though she could see she was distressing them.

"Fine, far as we know."

Claire decided to tell them more. They would need to know it sometime. "We're not sure how your son came to die. It looks like someone tied him into his car and drowned him. But there is a chance he could have done it to himself." There, it was out in the world. She watched the two parents' faces sag.

"No, I don't think so," Mr. Owens said first.

"Not our Buck."

"He wasn't always the smartest kid in school, but he was certainly the happiest."

"What if Stephanie had broken up with him?" Claire asked.

Mrs. Owens waved her hand as if it were her turn to speak. "No way. Buck didn't abide by taking your own life. He was raised good in the church. He might have moped for a while. I've seen him do that. But he would never kill himself. I don't want to hear no more talk about it."

✦

They had the whole week off school, and Meg was glad she was only halfway through the week. Her mother had let her go to the special school down in Stockholm, where she got to play with other kids and help out with the teacher. The kids were pretty little, but she had loved every minute of it. The teacher, whose name was Crystal, made her feel very special. Every afternoon she got to read to the kids.

Even helping Crystal clean up after the kids left was fun. Then they would sit in her big kitchen and drink tea and eat cookies. It made her think that maybe she would want to be a teacher when she grew up. Maybe she would start her own school.

When her mother came to get her, she jumped into the car and asked, "Hey, Mom, maybe you could home-school me and I could work for Crystal three days a week, or something like that?"

Her mother turned out of the driveway and then drove down to the highway before saying, quietly but firmly, "There are child labor laws."

"What?"

"You need to go to school."

"Lots of the kids around here are home-schooled."

"You are not one of them. I am not one of those parents. Those families have two parents, and one or both of them work at home. There's just me, and I go to work every day, in case you hadn't noticed."

"Rich could help."

"No, he couldn't."

"I bet he would if I asked."

"Aside from the fact that he would do anything for you, you are not his responsibility. Plus, he doesn't have the time."

"During the winter he does."

"Meg, even if he could, we would not ask him." Mom was talking in her preachy voice. "He's a friend of ours. You don't take advantage of friends. You only ask them for help when you really need it. Understand?"

"But I bet I could go to some of my friends' houses and be home-schooled with them. Like the Swansons."

"Even if you could, which I'm not so sure of, I don't really believe in it. I think you should go to school. I think you learn things at school that you won't at home. I think it's good for you, especially as an only child, to be with a lot of other kids. But I'll tell you the most important reason I won't home-school you—"

"What?" Meg asked.

"I think the other kids in school need you. You are smart. You might be one of the smartest kids there. They need smart kids in school. It helps everybody."

"But, Mom, I hate school."

Her mom looked over at her and then said with real surprise in her voice, "You do? When did that happen?"

Meg knew she could not tell her mother about her problems with Mr. Turner. Mom had enough problems on her plate. "I don't know. Just happened. Too much work and not enough play."

"You're probably right about that. Maybe we should be doing a little more playing at home. I think we'll be able to go ice-skating very soon. Maybe tonight."

"Yes, Mom. Please, please, promise me, whatever happens, we get to go ice-skating tonight."

"Well, I will say this—if we get the house cleaned up, the table set for tomorrow, the cranberry sauce made, then we can go down and check the ice."

"I know it's safe. Everybody was talking about it today. Sven is going to clear the ice this year for an ice-skating rink right by the park. That's what Crystal said."

"Sven sure is a nice man."

✦

Snooper whined at the door.

"Yes, we'll go outside."

At the word *outside*, Snooper stood up on his back legs and twirled.

"How about a walk? I think we both could use a walk."

An even more important word, *walk*. The twirling continued, and now the tongue came out.

Stephanie walked over to the hook by the door where she hung the nice new black leather leash she had bought for Snooper at the company store. She had bundled up in two long-sleeved shirts, a sweater, her Packers jacket, a polar fleece hat, old Red Wing boots with two pairs of socks underneath, and flannel-lined jeans. Snooper needed to get dressed too. Looking out the window at the thermometer on the tree, she saw it had dropped to near zero again. It was a brisk one.

"Come here, Snooper. You need to calm down." She had also bought him a polar fleece coat at the store with a cutout in the bottom so he could pee without getting it wet. She made him put his two front feet into it, then Velcroed it over his back. It had a high red collar and a green body. With his heavy fur under that, he should stay pretty warm.

"Okay, let's go." She turned the porch light on and stepped outside. The stillness of the woods settled on her. Then she saw what was making it so quiet. Snow was coming down. It must have just started. A sifting of white. Lovely, lovely snow. Inside her something grew, a feeling of hope and possibility. If this soft confection could fall from the sky and transform the world in an hour, surely she could take charge of her life and make it into one she would want.

Snooper pulled at his leash.

"Let's go down to the lake," she suggested, and again, the happy little dog danced.

They walked, and the snow fell, light, feathery snow that sailed out of the sky. Around the lampposts in the town, it seemed to swarm like bees around a hive. It started to accumulate on the sidewalks.

When they got to the town center, they turned down the street going to the park. No cars were parked on the street, no one was outside at all. The new Christmas decorations had been hung last week—large silver bells—and they moved gently in the snow. Everyone in town had contributed money toward the bells. Sven had worked hard to hang them up. He was so proud of them. He told her he had picked them out himself.

Down on the lake, Stephanie could see two figures out on the ice, one bigger than her and the other about half that size. She slowed her steps; she didn't really want to talk to anyone. She was leaving. It made no sense to try to get to know anyone. She was gone.

But she kept moving toward the lake. When Snooper saw the two people on the lake, he strained at his leash to go see them. He was a very friendly dog and liked to greet everyone. Stephanie kept a good hold on him. He would have to be disappointed.

When she was close to the edge of the lake, she could see who was out on the ice. It was the woman deputy, Claire Watkins, and her daughter. Stephanie wasn't sure what the little girl's name was, but she sure was cute. She had on a pair of skates and was trying her darnedest to move around on the ice. Her ankles were bending, and her skates were slipping out from under her. Down she went.

"Mom, that's ten. I've fallen down ten times so far."

"I would have broken every bone in my body," Claire said. She had on big boots and was sliding around close to her daughter, but not trying to catch her when she fell. That was probably a good idea. That way her daughter would learn more quickly not to fall—there would be incentive.

Stephanie stood close to them and watched. Snooper started to whine, so she picked him up and cuddled him. He snuggled down into her arms and hid his head in the crook of her sleeve.

She wanted to have a daughter. One that she would protect so that no man would ever hurt her.

The snow kept falling.

Stephanie remembered when she had told the policeman that her boyfriend had hit her. "So move out," he had said.

"I don't want to leave him."

"Then I can't help you."

When Jack had broken her arm, she had gone back in to file charges. She went to the same policeman because she thought he would remember her. He had.

"It's your own fault," he had told her.

She had left without filing. She knew she would get no help there.

She could step out onto the ice and say that someone was trying to kill her. She could tell this Claire about all that had gone wrong in her life. But Claire had a daughter, and they were having fun skating. Thanksgiving was tomorrow. No one wanted to hear about her problems. Claire would probably blame Stephanie too. Tell her that if she would have only thought more highly of herself, this would have never happened.

Stephanie had only seen Buck skate once. When she had first started to get to know him, he had invited her to go watch him play hockey. She had been astounded at how graceful he had been on the ice. The ugly duckling became a swan in front of her eyes. But the ice had betrayed him in the end. He had sunk under the ice. It had not held him and let him fly that one last time.

Tears and snow mixed on her face. She gripped Snooper and turned away from the lake. She needed to pack. It was time to get ready to leave.

10

THE big bird was cold, ugly, and awkward. It lay on the kitchen counter like a lump of lard. It was seven o'clock in the morning, and Claire would rather have been in bed. The stuffing was almost ready to go in the turkey. She had precooked the liver and onions on the stove, then folded in the bread crumbs and water. The resultant mélange wasn't particularly appetizing, a gray, soggy mess.

Steven had always cooked the turkey—when he was alive. The memory of him in their old kitchen shot through her. Sometimes she missed her dead husband so much the feeling threatened to weaken her knees and tumble her to the floor. She remembered Steven making coffee, humming in the kitchen as he manhandled the turkey into a roaster and slammed it into the oven. He loved cooking big chunks of meat, a beef slab or rack of lamb or humongous turkey.

Claire had bought a twenty-pounder. According to *The Joy of Cooking*, this bird would have to cook at least six hours and then sit for another half hour before you carved it. She figured if she got it in by eight, they could easily eat by four.

Rich said his mother would like to leave by six so she could get home before her bedtime.

Claire reviewed the menu in her mind: she'd done the cranberry molds last night, and they were chilling in the fridge, Bridget would bring the relish, Rich's mom the chestnut dressing, the turkey would go in soon, Meg would make the pumpkin pie this morning when she got up. Claire had yet to make mashed potatoes, wild rice, and green beans with almonds. She had bought rolls from Le Pain Perdu. They were all set to go. They wouldn't go hungry, that was for sure.

If only Rich's mother wasn't coming. If it wasn't for that, Claire would be totally relaxed. Come to that, she'd be sleeping. They would have eaten at a more fashionable hour.

The phone rang as she was cramming the stuffing inside the turkey. She knew it could only be one person. "Almost in," she answered the phone, cradling it on her shoulder so she could keep stuffing.

"You or the turkey?" Rich asked.

Claire laughed. She blessed the man who could make her laugh as she was elbow deep inside a turkey.

"I thought you'd be up."

"Wish you were here," she said.

"Will be soon. I'm heading out to get the matriarch. Hope the drive isn't too bad. It's supposed to snow all day long, according to the weather station."

"It's beautiful."

"Mom might have to stay with me tonight, if we get too much snow."

Claire looked out the window. It was still dark out, but under the streetlights she could see how deep the snow was on the road. Everything looked clean and perfect in this almost completely black-and-white landscape.

"Have the snowplows been by on the highway?" she asked him.

"Not yet. But they should be soon. Don't envy those guys."

"Drive careful. I hope you don't get stuck in Rochester with your mom."

"We'd probably have Spam for dinner. She still has that around as a remnant from the cold-war mentality."

They said their good-byes and hung up.

Claire faced the turkey. She hoisted it up and plopped it into the roaster. It just fit. It hadn't even occurred to her that it might not. She smeared it with butter and salted and peppered it. A short prayer for the perfect turkey to save the day. The oven was preheated. In it went.

She grabbed the cardamom roll she had heated in the oven, poured herself another cup of coffee, perched on a stool at her counter, and looked out the window. The snow fell so quietly. Everything glowed in its covering. Light showed faintly in the east, over the bluffs, and gently through the snow. The day had started. It would bring what it would bring.

Mom said she could do it totally herself. She had even given Meg the kitchen and was lounging in the bathtub taking a soaking bath. "As long as someone's doing something, I can relax," she had told Meg before she left the room.

Meg did not want to disappoint her mother. This pie had to be perfect. Mom had already made the crust, chilling in the fridge. The one rule Mom had was that Meg should wait until her mother was done with the bath to put the pie in the oven. "I don't want you to burn yourself," she said.

The way to start, Meg decided, was to put everything out so you could see it all. She got her favorite bowl, a big red one that would be way big enough to hold the pie filling. Mom had already opened the can of pumpkin, and she set that next to the bowl. Then she lined up the spices: nutmeg, cinnamon, mace, and allspice. Her favorite was nutmeg—it smelled the way she thought a fairy might smell.

She got the salt from the stovetop, and then she needed

the sugar. A small bowl of sugar sat next to the stove. The chunks looked kinda big, but she was sure they would melt in the pie filling. She grabbed that and set it next to all her other ingredients. Then she got the measuring devices. She loved the silver chain of spoons, one slightly bigger than the next, and how they all fit together. So sweet.

Now she was ready to go. It was more exciting doing it all by yourself. Total responsibility. She wished Mr. Turner would allow her that. If she home-schooled, she could really learn to cook. Her friend Janie, who home-schooled, did all the baking for her family. She was Meg's same age, and she made chocolate chip cookies and pies and even cakes that she frosted and everything.

First Meg lifted up the pumpkin can and turned it upside down. Nothing happened. She gave it a couple of good, hard thumps on the bottom, and the orange goop came sliding out. Plop! Gross, she thought. She wondered what it tasted like plain. Meg stuck her finger in and took a taste. Really gross! Like bad baby food.

She was so excited her little cousin was coming over today. Maybe Bridget would let her hold Rachel. She knew she could do it. She was nearly the age where she could babysit. In another year or two, she would probably be baby-sitting Rachel. What a blast! Rachel would really be like her little sister.

Then Meg wondered about Rich's mother. She was picturing her like the Wicked Witch of the West from *The Wizard of Oz*. Her grandmother June was nice and always smelled like a flower. But Meg could tell that her mother was nervous about Rich's mother coming and thought maybe it was because she wasn't very nice. Meg would be on her best behavior.

Carefully Meg started measuring in the spices. They made the mixture turn a darker color. It looked better, more like pumpkin pie should look. Then she cracked in the egg and mixed in the milk. She added the salt and then the sugar.

She thought of trying the mixture again, but decided it would taste so much better when it was all cooked together. Like a chemistry experiment.

"Mom," she yelled. "It's all ready."

"What?" her mother yelled back.

Meg ran to the door of the bathroom. "Can I come in?"

"Sure, sweetie."

Meg opened the door and, as she stepped into the room, was enveloped in the good-smelling mist from her mother's bath. Her mother's hair was up high on her head in a ponytail, and her body was stretched out in the tub.

She didn't see her naked very often, but her mother wasn't shy or anything. She walked around in her bra and underpants if it was warm out, sometimes. She didn't always close the door when she was going to the bathroom. But her mother's body still surprised her—it was so soft looking with those round breasts. Meg knew she was going to get some, but she didn't quite believe it.

"I'm done, Mom."

"Great. I'll be out in another minute or two. Thanks for helping out, Meg. I couldn't do it without you."

"Do you need me to scrub your back?"

"Oh, not today. I think I've soaked all the dirt off me." Her mother stepped up out of the water and wrapped a towel around her body.

"Hey, Mom, can we make ourselves beautiful for the company?" Meg knew just the outfit she wanted to wear—her red velvet top and black skinny pants.

"I think that would be a great idea." Her mother leaned over her, warm and wet smelling, and kissed her on the forehead.

"I tasted the pumpkin."

"That's a good idea when you're cooking, to taste as you go along."

"It didn't taste very good."

"It's going to be delicious."

The snow was still coming down. Stephanie watched it for a
moment as she packed a big duffel with clothes. Thank God
the snowplow had just gone by on the highway. At least she
would be able to get out of here. If she would have had to stay
one more day, she would have lost her mind. As it was she was
hardly sleeping anymore, hearing sounds in the night.

Stephanie was only taking two of everything—like Noah
loading up the Ark—two nightgowns, two jeans, two T-shirts,
two sweaters, two pairs of shoes, two shirts. But she decided
to take a week's worth of underclothes. She packed enough
food so she wouldn't have to stop for a day or two. She packed
a jug of water and put a huge bag of Snooper's food in the
trunk of the car. If need be, she could eat that. She had nib-
bled on it at work—it wasn't bad.

Her weaving she put into the backseat of the car. She
made a bed for Snooper on the floor of the passenger seat out
of an old afghan that her mother had crocheted for her. When
they got settled, it would be nice to have the afghan with her
to put on her new bed.

Stephanie would contact her mother eventually, but she
wouldn't tell her where she was. Not for a long, long time.

Jack hadn't stopped by to see her, nor had he called. He
often stepped back from her after a bad burst of violence. She
truthfully thought he didn't quite know what he had done, or
he was able quickly to forget the reality of his offense. But he
needed some time to do it. Even when they had lived together, he would walk around like he didn't see her for a
while. If he looked at her, he would have been forced to face
the evidence of his work.

She wished she could completely hate him. She was absolutely terrified of him, but in the core of her there was some
part that still wanted him, that still believed she could change
him. Maybe she would always have that. But if she got an
ocean between them, it would be harder to act on it.

Snooper was sitting on top of one of her piles of clothes.
He didn't want to be left behind. She felt like she could do

what she was doing—running far, far away—because of the dog. She wasn't as alone as she had been. She had something to take care of.

The one time she had gotten pregnant, Jack had blown up and beat her so bad that she had miscarried. She tried not to think about it too much. Part of her had been so relieved. How could she bring a child into a household with this violent man? How could she protect it when she couldn't even take care of herself? She was quite sure he had kicked her in the stomach on purpose.

Her hands shook, thinking about it. Time to go.

She carried down the last duffel bag. She was leaving the whole house full of furniture. She was also leaving a note telling the landlord to keep the damage deposit for December's rent. She didn't need him trying to track her down too. She had left a message on the voice mail at work, telling her boss that she quit. She had no mail coming that she needed forwarded.

No trace. She was about to disappear.

She went back into the house one last time. She would miss this place. A view of the lake, good walks, nice neighbors. Fort St. Antoine had been a good place for her to live. She had even thought she might be able to get enough work doing her rugs that she could make a go of it. But it was not to be.

After scooping Snooper up, she did one last walk-through of the house. She picked up the earrings that Jack had given her for Christmas many years ago, carried them into the bathroom, and flushed them down the toilet.

She had over a thousand dollars in her pocket. She had a fake ID that she had bought a few years ago.

"Let's go, little guy," she said to Snooper.

His body shook as he tried to wag his tail.

She locked the door and walked to the car, which she had left running. It would be warm for Snooper that way. She put him into his little bed on the floor, even though she suspected he would spend most of the time in the car sitting on her lap, looking out the window. She gave him a treat.

Then she backed out of the driveway. Too late, she realized that the snowplows had sealed off the end of it. She hit the white wall they had left behind and tried to drive through, only digging her car deeper into the huge snowbank.

She tried to rock the car by hitting the gas and then putting it in reverse, but it wouldn't move.

She was stuck.

11

S HE tried to get people to call her Beatrice when she first
met them, but after a while everyone seemed to want to
call her Bea. She didn't like being a letter of the alpha-
bet, a buzzing little creature that gathered nectar, a verb form.
She wanted to be the lover of Dante. But no one else wanted
to give her that.

"Introduce me as Beatrice," she told Rich when he came
to pick her up. "Oh, the snow, should we really be doing this?"
she asked him as she bundled into her black cashmere coat
with the white ermine collar.

"You look lovely, Mom. I will introduce you as Beatrice.
Don't worry. The roads were fine. I just drove them."

"But I have packed a small overnight bag in case I am
forced to stay at your house." Beatrice pointed to her little
carry case, sitting next to the door.

Rich leaned over and picked it up. "Good idea."

"I thought it wise."

"You are nothing if you are not wise."

She stepped out the door with him and locked it behind, checking it twice. "You humor me, Rich."

"Of course I do. You are my mother. It's my job."

She had raised her son well. Even though she had married beneath her, married a man she loved dearly and never minded the sacrifice she had made for him—and a sacrifice it had been: killing fowl with her bare hands, cooking for large groups of people, rising at an ungodly hour to feed the livestock—even though Rich had been raised on a farm, she had done a good job with him. He had very nice manners and was good to his mother.

"I hope I will like this new woman in your life," she said as Rich handed her into the car. She was worried that the woman wouldn't like her. His ex-wife had hated Beatrice. No matter what she said, she had planted her foot firmly in her mouth with that woman, who seemed to take even compliments as criticism. Beatrice vowed she would try hard today to be gracious.

"I'm sure you will."

"Sometimes your taste in women has been questionable."

"But that's all in the past."

"I do hope so, Rich." She flipped down the mirror in the visor and looked at herself. Her lipstick was on straight, and there were no traces of it on her teeth. She would just avoid looking at the wrinkles. She had slept so poorly last night, fretting about the long drive ahead of her and the huge dinner. She fluffed her white hair, but with no humidity it had fallen a little flat. "But a policewoman?"

"Even the criminals adore her. You'll see."

"Who else will be there?"

"Well, I wanted to talk to you about that. There will be her daughter, Meg, who is a very bright child, and then her sister, Bridget, will be there, and her young daughter."

"How young?" Beatrice asked suspiciously.

"Well, quite young."

"Yes?"

Rich started the car and drove out of her underground parking lot and into the falling snow. "Rachel was born more than three weeks ago."

"Dear God, a newborn." Beatrice felt herself cringe. Babies never seemed to like her. They always cried when she held them. She was afraid she would drop them. No proper conversation could take place when one was around.

"Mom, you managed with me."

"Yes, but I had to. It was the only way to get you to a respectable age. Why do you think I had no more children?"

"I know. You've told me many times."

"I will do my best."

They drove awhile in silence. But finally Beatrice tired of staring at the falling snow and turned on the classical music station. It added depth to the landscape. A little Bach, rather tinkly, but good.

"What are you thinking of doing with this Claire?"

"What do you mean?"

"Will you marry her?"

"Might. Don't know that she'll have me, but I will probably ask her at some point. But not for quite a while, I think. She's still recovering from her last marriage."

"And what happened?"

"I told you, Mom. Her husband was killed."

He probably had told her. How could she have forgotten that? Killed, my goodness. "That is drastic."

"She lived up in the Cities then. That's one of the reasons she moved to the country. To get away from all that violence."

"What will she and I find to talk about? I know nothing about murder and mayhem."

"She's just started quilting. You could ask her about that."

"Quilting. I didn't know anyone did that anymore."

"Mom, you're a snot."

"Well, darling, someone needs to raise the level of society these days." Beatrice leaned her head back. She really

hadn't slept at all well. Her eyes closed on their own, and
the last thing she heard was the end of the Bach piece, fad-
ing in her head like bits of snow sparkling in the wind. Tin
kly.

Then Rich was shaking her gently and saying, "Mother,
we're here."

Beatrice sat up. She felt so unprepared. "Don't manhan-
dle me, Rich. There's really no need."

He stepped back and waited for her to gather herself together. "Have you got the chestnut dressing?"

"Mom, you never gave it to me. Is it in your carry case?"

"No, I would never put it in there. I must have left it on
the kitchen table. Rich, what should we do?"

"It'll be fine. They won't know what they're missing."

"I can't believe I've gone and left that behind. I worked so
hard on it." Everyone always loved her chestnut dressing.
How could she have forgotten it? She got out of the car, and
Rich took her arm.

They walked up a shoveled path to the front door of a
small white clapboard house. At their knock, she could hear
feet running inside the house, and she braced herself. When
the door opened, a small girl's face smiled up at them with
lipstick smeared across it. The girl was wearing a velvet top
that matched her lipstick, and her mother came and stood behind her.

Oh, her son had gone and found himself a beauty. The
woman was tall and full figured, with dark hair that she was
wearing in a low roll. A white blouse and black velvet pants
looked very smart on her.

"Mrs. Haggard, we're so glad you could come," the
woman said.

"Please call me Beatrice," Beatrice said as she stretched
out her hand.

"What a lovely name," the woman said. "I will call you
that if you will call me Claire."

"Are you as clear as your name?" Beatrice asked her.

"I try to be." Claire pointed down at the girl who was standing next to her. "This is my daugher, Meg. She's been waiting very hard for you to come."

"I'm pretending you're my grandmother today," Meg said.

"Oh, you are?" Beatrice was surprised. "I've never had a grandchild."

Meg wrinkled her nose. "You haven't? You look like you're old enough to have one."

Rich reached over and tousled Meg's hair. "Age isn't the only prerequisite."

"May I touch your coat?" Meg asked.

"I suppose you may." Beatrice leaned over and let Meg stroke her collar. "It's ermine. Winter ermine, they turn pure white, you know."

"No, I didn't know that. So they blend into the snow?"

"Yes, so they blend in." Beatrice remembered her hostess gift. "I have something for you and your mother." She unzipped her carry case and pulled out her present. She had left it in a brown paper bag but put a big red bow on it.

Claire undid the bow, reached into the bag, and pulled out the large, dark bulb. Beatrice realized it looked rather awful. She should have potted it up. What had she been thinking?

"What is that shriveled thing?" Meg asked.

"It's an amaryllis. It will be a thing of beauty in a month or so." Beatrice took the bulb from Claire's hand and showed it to Meg. "You see this little green shoot? It will turn into a big stalk, and then a flower will explode from the end. This variety is called Picotee. They are my favorite. And I have a long history with amaryllis. It produces a glorious white flower just tipped with red."

"Oh," Meg's face lit up. "Like a Kleenex dipped in blood."

Beatrice was nonplussed. It didn't happen to her very often. What kind of life was this child leading?

Claire also looked aghast. "Meg, what made you think of that?"

"I had a bloody nose the other day."

"Well, that's enough of that talk." Claire reprimanded the child. "It sounds lovely, Beatrice. I'm sure we will enjoy it."

Bridget looked at her watch. She had told Claire she would be there by two, and it was almost three. She had just driven through Pepin and would soon be to Fort St. Antoine. The snow was slowing her down. Surely Claire would understand.

Rachel was sleeping, the little brat. She always slept in the car. What Bridget should do was to get Chuck to drive them both around so she could get some sleep too.

She had a bag full of three kinds of olives, two kinds of pickles, and Ziploc bags full of cut-up carrots and celery. It would have to do as the relish dish. She had found a great old relish tray from the sixties, lime green with starbursts. She thought it would be festive for the occasion.

As she slowed to come into town, she noticed that someone was stuck in their driveway. She slowed down more and saw that it was a woman, standing by her car. Bridget couldn't just drive past her. Maybe she needed help.

She slowed the car down and rolled down the window, hoping the cold air wouldn't wake up Rachel. "Do you need some help?"

The blond woman looked over at her and said, "No, thank you. I called a neighbor. He should be on his way soon. Don't worry about it."

"Were you going someplace for Thanksgiving?" Bridget asked, feeling sorry for her day ruined.

"No, not exactly." The blond woman was holding something wrapped in an afghan. "I just need to get out of here."

"Do you have a baby?" Bridget asked.

"No," the woman lifted off part of the blanket, and the head of a small dog peeked out. "I have Snooper."

Just then Rachel let out a shriek.

"Do you have a baby?"

"I do. I better go. She won't stop screaming until I pick her up. Happy Thanksgiving."

The woman waved as she drove away. Bridget wanted to try to remember to mention the woman's predicament to Claire, but when she got to the house, there was so much going on with unloading the baby that she forgot all about it.

Claire came running out and took the wailing Rachel. "She's getting big."

"I know, and mouthy."

"Just like her mom."

"I'm sorry I'm late."

"Not to worry."

"Is everyone here?"

"Yes," Claire whispered. "The queen has arrived."

"How's it going?"

"This woman has watched too much PBS. She thinks that there is such a thing as *Upstairs, Downstairs* in America, and she's upstairs and all the rest of us are downstairs."

"Oh, great. That will make me the scullery maid."

Claire leaned over and kissed her on the cheek. "I'm so glad you're here."

Bridget felt her love for her sister. "We haven't been together on Thanksgiving since Dad died."

"Too long."

Bridget thrust her grocery bag into the air. "Lead on to battle."

When she met Mrs. Haggard, or Beatrice as she wanted to be called, Bridget warmed to her. She was a tight, tall woman, handsome and nervous. Bridget thought she had a lot of backbone but wasn't always sure of herself. It made her caustic. Bridget put Rachel in Meg's lap, curled up next to the two girls on the couch, and watched Claire and Beatrice converse in the kitchen.

Beatrice stood as if overseeing everything and questioned Claire. "How are you enjoying working for a sheriff's department in this small county? Is it quite different than working in the city?"

"Oh, my, yes," Claire answered as she mashed the potatoes. "The biggest difference is the slower pace of work. I am very happy about that. I get to spend more time with my daughter. But the other thing that is different is that I know so many of the people I'm working for. I will know most everyone in the county soon. It gives it a very different feel. I'm defending and protecting my neighbors."

"What a nice way to put it," Beatrice said. "Are you making gravy?"

"Rich's got it going."

Bridget watched Claire try to do it all and was glad that Meg was holding Rachel and that she got to sit quietly on the couch and drink a glass of wine. It was only her third glass of wine since the baby was born, a special occasion.

"Any big cases?" Beatrice asked.

"Not on a holiday," Claire answered, then said, "Everybody to the table."

Rich lifted up the silver platter with an enormous turkey on it and carried it to the wonderfully set table. Claire had used their parents' good china, rimmed in gold. Bridget stuffed pillows around Rachel on the couch and hoped she would sleep for a while so she could be adult and eat at the table.

Jack watched the snow move across the road like a hail of white bullets. He had braved the storm because he decided he needed to check on Stephanie. He hadn't heard from her for a few days. He figured they had things to talk about. And, after all, it was a holiday. Family was family.

Bring her a little Thanksgiving cheer. See that she was doing all right. He had bought a bottle of champagne and hoped that she might be cooking a turkey. She would be surprised to see him. They had their problems once in a while, but she understood him in a way that no one else did. He needed her.

When he slowed to turn into her driveway, he saw that her old beater car was stuck at the end of her driveway, packed to the gills. Then she stepped out of her house, holding something in her arms. What the hell was she up to now?

He parked his car as far off the road as he could manage. The snow was letting up a bit. Visibility wasn't too bad. He'd leave his parking lights on.

"What's going on?" he asked her.

She came running down from the house when she saw the car and then slowed when she saw it was him. As he walked toward her, he saw that she was carrying a small dog in her arms. Didn't she know he hated dogs? Whiney, yippy curs. Who had she been waiting for? Another boyfriend?

"Jack, get out of here!" she screamed at him.

He ignored her anger. Maybe they could move past it today. "I see you need some help."

"Someone is coming any minute."

"I brought you something." He held out the bottle. "I thought we could have a good time."

She clutched the dog. "No, not today."

He walked right up to her, close enough to see the wind whip tears into her eyes. What was the matter with her? She had always been such a scaredy-cat. "Let me see the dog." He reached out to take it, and she pulled back from him. He hated when she did that, pulled back as if he was going to hit her.

"No. You get away from us. I know what you did with Buck. And I will tell the cops if you touch me."

"What're you talking about? Me and Buckie needed to get to know each other. That's all."

"I hate you."

"What're you up to, babe?"

She tried to turn away, but he grabbed her arm. He had

the bottle of champagne in the other hand. She wouldn't say anything.

"Do I have to beat it out of you?" he asked.

She bent over and set the little dog down and yelled, "Run, Snooper, run!" The dog tore up the path to the house.

Jack just wanted to talk to her, but she was striking out at him, trying to get away. He kept a good grip on her arm so she couldn't pull away from him. He had wanted to have dinner with her. Now it didn't seem possible. If she would only hold still. The burn ignited. He hated her doing this to him. She had to stop. He didn't bother unwrapping the bottle of champagne. The blows were muffled by the brown paper bag.

The first half of the dinner had gone fine. Rich had had trouble carving the turkey, but everyone had teased him, and it had given them something to laugh and talk about.

Then Meg dumped a cranberry mold that hadn't molded on her new velvet top. Claire could tell by the way she tightened her lips that she was about to cry. She looked up at her mom, and her lips quivered. "It will wash out, Meggy."

"But, Mom, it's sticky."

Then Rachel started to scream from the next room.

Bridget lifted herself up from the table with the movements of a much older woman. She looked as if she was about ready to fall over from sleep deprivation. She picked up Rachel from her bed of pillows and brought her back to the table. The baby writhed in her mother's arms and wept.

Beatrice's face spelled deep disapproval. But she said nothing, just scraped the tines of her fork across her plate to get the last of her stuffing.

Rich tried to smooth things over by asking his mother about her weekly bridge game.

"Oh, no one wants to hear about that," Beatrice snapped. "The game will die out when my generation passes on. Nobody plays it anymore. And it's a fine, intelligent game. No one wants to take the time to learn it. They would rather watch TV or play those stupid Nintendo games."

It wasn't that Claire didn't like Rich's mother; it was that she found her exhausting. She wasn't sure what role she was supposed to play with her, and she felt as if she was struggling to make conversation.

Everyone finished eating in relative silence. Even Rachel calmed down long enough so Bridget could finish her food.

Meg jumped up as soon as she was finished and asked if she could get the pie.

"Wait until everyone is finished, sweetie."

Rich stood up. "I'm done too. Let's go into the kitchen and get that whipped cream ready."

A few minutes later, her darling daughter proudly brought out the pumpkin pie so everyone could see it before it was cut. Rich came behind her with a big bowl of whipped cream.

"My, that looks nice," Beatrice said.

Meg beamed. "Mom, can you cut it? I don't want to ruin it."

Claire stood and cut the first piece and graciously gave it to Beatrice after Rich had smacked a large dollop of whipped cream on it. Then they served everyone else. Claire sat down and took a bite of her pie. Something was very wrong with the pie. It was not sweet at all.

Meg held her mouth open and screamed, "Mom."

"Spit it out on your plate."

Meg did as she was told.

"Did you put sugar in the pie filling?"

"Yes."

"What sugar?"

"The stuff in the bowl by the stove."

"Oh, dear, that's salt."

Meg started to cry. Claire felt like joining her. Rachel did. Beatrice pushed her pie plate away.

Bridget, who had not said much the whole meal, stood up

and plopped Rachel in Beatrice's lap. Claire wasn't sure who looked more surprised—the old woman or the baby. Beatrice looked as if someone had dumped the rest of the pumpkin pie on her lap. Her hands flew up as if she didn't want to get them dirty.

"I can't take any more crying. I need to sleep." Bridget left the room.

Beatrice didn't seem to know where to put her hands. The baby curled up against her and looked as if it was about to slide onto the floor. Beatrice gingerly put a hand behind its head and then began to jiggle her knees.

Miraculously, the baby stopped crying. Meg sniffled. Beatrice gently jostled the baby and then picked up her spoon. She looked at Meg with a smile. "You know what one of my favorite desserts is?" she asked.

"What?"

"Whipped cream." She proceeded to pile mounds on her plate and Meg's.

Then the phone rang. Claire looked at Rich, who shrugged and shook his head. She answered it.

Claire recognized Sven Slocum's voice, even though he didn't identify himself as he tried to get out his words. She could tell he was frightened. "She might be dead. You have to come. It's bad."

12

Claire had never seen anything like it: a brilliant splash of red blood cut across the new fallen snow like bright carnelian paint splashed across a freshly gessoed canvas. The battered woman looked as if she had been caught making angels in the snow—her feet splayed apart, her arms flung wide—but her broken face told another story. It was smashed, the nose twisted, the lips bruised, the eyes battered. Claire could hardly recognize the woman as Stephanie, but the pale blond hair tucked under a cap gave her away.

And then on top of the woman sat the small brown-and-white dog, shivering and watchful. As they approached, it started to growl.

Sven stood near, wringing his hands. "He won't let me get near her. I've tried, and he barks."

"He's only a little dog," Claire said, slowly inching toward the woman.

"But he bites," Sven said.

Rich told her to stop. "I'll get him to come to me. It'll be better." He sat down on the snow. "Come here, guy." He patted the snow in front of him. "You've done your job. Now, come." The last word he said very forcefully, and the little dog jumped down off Stephanie's motionless body and begrudgingly walked up to Rich. Rich scooped him up and told him he was a good dog.

Claire allowed herself a moment to think of Rich's reaction to this scene—she was sure he had never seen anything this gruesome before—and then moved right in on Stephanie. She hoped the EMTs would be here soon. She had called the ambulance from her house before she left.

Please let her be alive, she prayed. The eyes looked the worst, swollen shut with dark blue mottling all around the hollow.

Claire remembered the abused woman in Minneapolis who had been blinded by her husband. He had taken a knife to her eyes, tried to carve them out, and left two gaping holes in her head. So she knew it could be worse.

The bone of Stephanie's nose looked crushed and crooked. Claire figured that's where most of the blood had come from. Bending close, she thought she detected a breath. A finger to the carotid gave her a weak but steady response.

"Stephanie," she said and nudged the woman. A faint groan whistled out into the cold, quiet air.

"Rich, she's still alive. Go to the house and get blankets. We don't want to lose her to shock."

Claire looked around at the crime scene. Give it up, she told herself, for soon it will be polluted with more footprints than you can paw through. Snow was covering the tracks of whoever had been here. She would do the best she could, once they got Stephanie safely in an ambulance, but at the moment she had to concentrate on the life of this woman and forget about her assailant.

She couldn't help but ask Sven, "Did you see anyone, Sven? How did you happen to come here?"

He stood right behind her. "Is she going to be okay? Such a nice woman, Stephanie is."

"I don't know. Can you answer my questions?"

"She called me a couple hours ago. Left a message on my machine. Her car wouldn't start. I wasn't home. I had gone to some friends to eat turkey and all. When I got home about twenty minutes ago I got her message and came right away. This is how I found her. No one was here. I think whoever did it parked just off the road. Past where my car is."

"I'll check there later. Thanks."

Rich brought the blankets, having left the dog in the house. They covered her as best they could without moving her. Claire looked up at Rich. She had started to count on him. "Is there anything else we can do to get her warm without moving her?"

"Rub her hands. Get her to feel your contact. It might bring her out."

Claire took off the black woollen glove Stephanie was wearing, took her small white hand in hers, and rubbed it. Claire didn't know if she believed Rich that it would make the woman warmer, but it did give her something to do, and she did believe that human touch could bring people back from the brink of death.

"Stephanie, we're here. You're going to be all right." Claire heard the words come out of her mouth automatically. She hoped they were true.

Another truck pulled up at the end of the driveway, and a big man burst out of it. As he came closer, Claire saw that it was Clay Burnes, the emergency medical technician who had also shown up at Buck's drowning. She hoped the ambulance would be close behind. They needed to get her out of here.

"We meet again," he said as he came up to her.

"Unfortunately." She stood up and allowed Clay to get in close to Stephanie. As he checked her over, Claire filled him in on what she knew. He was nodding his head and indicating that he was getting good response from Stephanie. She groaned again and turned her head to the side.

"Do you know who did this?" he asked.

"No. Not yet."

"We can assume a guy," he stated.

Claire nodded.

"What did he use on her?" he asked.

"I don't know. Haven't had a chance to look. He might have taken it with him." Then she added, "Clay, this woman was Buck's girlfriend."

Clay looked up at her, his eyes wide and unblinking. "What the hell is going on here?"

The ambulance roared in, pushing its way through the plow drift across the end of the driveway. Two men jumped out of the vehicle, and one burst out of the back. Claire stepped back and watched as they circled Stephanie, working on her as Clay orchestrated their moves.

Rich had hated leaving Claire at Stephanie's, with blood all over the snow, and the woman carefully packed off to the hospital. Claire was left to tramp through the snow and see if anything had been left behind that would identify the bastard that had beaten up Stephanie. But someone had to get back to their guests.

Snooper whined on the seat next to him. Claire had told him the name of the dog before he left with it. Rich reached over and petted the little guy. He must be pretty upset—losing two owners in less than a week. Rich hoped Stephanie would be back on her feet soon, but he didn't count on it— she had looked so horrible.

When he saw that the dog was still shaking, he unzipped his jacket, put the dog inside, and zipped it back up. The dog hunkered down into the jacket, not even his head showing.

The snow had all but stopped when Rich drove back up to

Claire's house to rescue Bridget and his mother. He pulled into the driveway and sat for a moment, trying to calm down. He felt like he wanted to slam his fist into a wall, into any man who would do that to a woman. How could Claire go on seeing that kind of stuff day after day?

Maybe she didn't see it that frequently down in Pepin County, but she must have seen it far too often in the Cities. Even down here, it happened. People ignored such abuse, thought it wasn't their business when their neighbors were beating up their wives and battering their kids.

It sickened him. He wanted to walk up the bluff and down and get it out of his system, but he had to go in and reassure his mother and Bridget that everything was all right. After all, it was Thanksgiving. Since the dog seemed comfortable, he left him inside his jacket and got out of the car.

When he walked into the house, the first thing that surprised him was the quiet. The second was that the kitchen was clean. Then he found his mother sitting on the couch, reading a book to Meg, who was already in her pajamas. The baby Rachel was sleeping, tucked in next to his mother, a bottle resting on her chest. Maybe she would make a good grandmother someday—if she ever got the chance.

When he asked where Bridget was, he was told she was still sleeping in the guest bedroom.

Meg looked up at him, pleased with herself. "Beatrice and I did the dishes. I wiped."

Rich walked up to his mother and kissed her forehead. "Good job, Mom."

"Someone had to make order out of all this. Tell Claire we improvised a little when we put the dishes away."

"We even changed the baby's diaper, and it was a poopy one."

"I remembered how," his mother said. "It's so easy now with those disposables. They have the tape built into them. What a breeze."

Rich wondered if maybe what his mother needed wasn't less responsibility, but more.

"Where's Claire?" Beatrice asked.

"She had to stay and do some work."

"Work?"

Rich didn't want to say more. "Yeah, finish things up." Snooper's head came popping out of the jacket. "Oh, I brought a friend home."

"For me?" Meg jumped off the couch and ran to see the dog.

Rich unzipped his coat and said, "No, Megsly. I'm sorry, but this dog has an owner that he loves very much. He's just visiting. But could you take him into the kitchen and get him a drink of water?"

He put the little dog down on the floor, and Meg and the dog touched noses. He had guessed they might be friends.

"Snooper is his name," Rich told her.

Meg called the dog, and the two of them ran off to the kitchen. Rich heard her turn on the faucet.

"Why is he visiting?" his mother asked.

"Because his owner had to go to the hospital."

"What happened, Rich?"

"A woman was beat up. It was bad." He thanked the Lord that he had never seen such a sight before. He hoped he would never see anything like it again.

His thoughts went to Claire, walking around in the snow. He wondered if he should think about asking her to quit her job.

The yellow tape was looped across the bottom of the driveway. Scott Lund had come from Pepin and taken as many pictures outside as he could, his flash lighting up the falling snow. She had been on the phone to the sheriff several times, coordinating how to handle the scene. He had agreed that the crime bureau could meet her there tomorrow morning. The snow kept falling, and it wasn't helping anything.

The snow was silently, constantly covering everything up—one of the attributes she most loved about it. The first snow coming in late fall, early winter, hid the damped-down weeds, the empty trees, the trash along the roadside, the dirt on everything. But now she was fighting it.

She tried to reconstruct the scene. She had gone into the house and walked through it carefully, touching nothing. It was hard to tell whether Stephanie had been leaving for good, but Claire guessed yes. She had packed the essentials. The car was stuffed to the brim. The crime lab could come into the house tomorrow, but she doubted that they would find anything. Claire didn't think any of the fight happened in the house. It was too neat; nothing looked thrown around.

In reconstructing the action, she imagined Stephanie down by her car, the man arriving on the scene, immediately guessing what she was up to, and going at her right there by the car.

That's why Claire was walking around outside. If she was going to find anything, it would be out here. It was dark, the only light coming from the porch. The snow gave off its own glow. Claire had a huge flashlight that she was flicking around the edges of the scene. Suddenly, something snapping in the wind caught her eye.

She walked a few steps into the forest. Caught in a pine tree was a paper bag. She lifted it up carefully and peeked in. A green bottle, smashed. As Claire examined it more carefully, she saw that it was a bottle of champagne, the price still on it—$12.99. Not a big spender, but maybe he couldn't get a more expensive bottle down along the river.

She carefully carried the bag with the champagne bottle to her car and put it in a box in the backseat. Then she sat on the edge of her seat with the car door open and watched the snow come down.

This wasn't really a storm. Maybe an accumulation of

four to five inches. Nothing that significant. Enough to get Stephanie stuck, but not enough to slow down the man who had come to court her with a bottle of champagne. What went on between the two of them that he had turned the bottle on her? How afraid must she have been, to pack up what she could stuff in her car and try to flee? How was this all tied into Buck's death? Was Stephanie covering for someone else, or had she killed Buck, and was she trying to get away before they figured it out?

Claire hoped she would get these answers the next time she saw Stephanie.

Her son was in love.

It was obvious. He wore it on his face whenever he looked at Claire, whenever he talked about her.

And she seemed like a good woman. She was raising a lovely daughter, had a devoted if slightly wacky sister, a nice house. She seemed like an average housemaker and a decent cook.

But she was a cop.

Beatrice tucked her head under the edge of the flannel sheets on the bed in the room where Aunt Agnes used to sleep. Rich was so careful about everything in his life. He made a good living at raising pheasants, he had his house all paid off, he kept everything simple and clean. How had he come to let this woman into his life?

Beatrice was happy for him, but also scared. This was the woman he wanted, and she wasn't sure they were a perfect match. Claire carried so much of the world on her shoulders. It might turn out to be too much for Rich to compete with.

13

C LAIRE called the hospital from her house before she
left for work. Late the night before she had gotten the
news that Stephanie was still unconscious, but stable.
The doctor who came to the phone to talk to her in the morning assured her that Stephanie was doing as well as could be
expected, but that they were going to need to do some repair
work, probably surgery, on her face.

"What happened to her?" he asked.

Claire thought it was quite clear. "Someone beat her up."

"With what, I mean? It might help us know the nature of
the damage."

"A champagne bottle wrapped in a paper bag."

She heard a loud sigh on the other end of the line. "What
a way to say Happy Thanksgiving."

"Exactly. What might she need surgery on?"

"I'm concerned about her eyes. It's hard to know how well
she's seeing right now, but it doesn't look good to me. And her
nose needs to be reset. I don't think she's breathing very well
out of it right now."

"Is she coherent?"

"Minimally. We've got her pretty doped up. She suffered a concussion, but that's the least of her problems."

"She's still in intensive care with restrictions on visitors?"

"Yes, and she'll continue to be there for at least the rest of the day, and I'm guessing the next day or two. The good news is she has no internal injuries other than the concussion that I can determine. The assault was focused on her head and face."

"That's the way the loved ones beat you up. Make you look bad to the rest of the world."

She had used the phone in her bedroom so Bridget and Meg wouldn't overhear her talking to the doctor. She didn't want them to know what had happened. Both of them were still nervous from their own traumas. Bridget had a nasty scar on her arm from a bullet hole; Meg still had bad dreams at night. They didn't need to be reminded that evil men roamed the world.

When she came downstairs, they were busy making oatmeal. Meg was teaching Bridget. "Keep stirring until you turn the heat down. That way it won't stick," Meg told her.

"Where's the wonder child?" Claire asked.

"She's fed, she's dry, she's yonder sleeping. I think she likes all the noise of people moving around her. Maybe it's too quiet at my house." Bridget pointed to the bundle of baby curled up on the couch between two pillows. "She just doesn't seem to like to go into her bedroom and sleep in her bed. She reminds me of myself—never wanting to miss anything that's going on."

Claire walked over and knelt down by the dark-haired infant. She hadn't had much time for her yesterday. Rachel pursed her lips, then made quiet smacking sounds, but kept sleeping. Claire felt the urge to reach out and touch her soft white cheeks, but resisted. A sleeping baby was just what they all needed right now. Bridget had a little more color in her face than when she showed up yesterday afternoon.

"So you're sure you don't mind being here today?"

Bridget looked at her. "Are you kidding? I've just had the best sleep since before the baby was born. Meg is teaching me how to cook. My husband is gone for another day. My darling child is sleeping. And the roads still aren't much good. You better believe I'm happy to stay put."

"So how did you think it went yesterday with Rich's mom, the noble Beatrice?" Claire asked.

"I would say you made an impression." Bridget laughed.

Claire couldn't argue with that.

Bridget walked into the living room to talk to her, leaving Meg to attend to the oatmeal. "Claire, I wanted to ask you about that woman yesterday. Was her car stuck in her driveway?"

Claire looked up at her sister. "How did you know?"

"I stopped and talked to her just before I got to your house."

"Why?"

"Because I saw her car was stuck."

"Was anyone there?"

"No. I asked if she needed help, but she said that she had called someone and they would be there shortly."

Claire left the two of them planning to make chocolate chip cookies in the afternoon. She had a strong desire to stay home and play house with the three favorite women in her life, but then she thought of Stephanie's face, grabbed her keys, and was out the door before she could think again.

Claire had arranged to meet with Clark Denforth from the crime bureau over at Stephanie Klaus's house at nine A.M. When she parked down the road, she saw that the snowplow had already been by. If there had been any remnants of tracks left by the assailant's car, they were gone now.

She reached into the back of the car and lifted out the box with the bagged champagne bottle in it. Perhaps they could lift prints off the bottle unless he kept his gloves on in the store when he bought it.

Clark Denforth parked right behind her car. She carried the box back to him. "An early Christmas present. Smashed champagne bottle." She put the box in the back of his car.

"Oh, champagne gives me a headache," he said, peering into the box to see what it contained.

"Assault weapon. I don't know what you're going to find here. We had quite a crew at the scene yesterday."

"How many?" Clark looked at her.

She counted. "Seven besides the assailant. Seven that I know of. Eight including the victim." Then she remembered Scott coming after everyone else had left to take photographs. "Oops, I mean nine."

"Then there is the snow."

"And the plows, which already wiped out the car tracks."

"Don't you just love winter." He walked up to the car that Claire had locked last night. She didn't think Stephanie's mess of possessions were worth much, but it was her job to secure them.

"I think they fought by the car. She was trying to leave, and he decided to clobber her," Claire told him.

Denforth walked around the car, then leaned under and patted the snow by the driver's side. "There's something under here. I can see the darkness through the snow." Carefully he wiped the snow away and uncovered a scarf, a dark brown scarf.

"A man's wool scarf," Claire said. "That's what it could be. It could belong to the assailant."

Looking it over carefully, Denforth corrected her, "A man's cashmere scarf."

Sven loaded his snowblower into the back of the truck and brought it down to the end of the park. His wife used to tease him that he'd be out blowing the snow off the sidewalk before it had even quit coming down. He did like his machines. Gave him something to do now that he was retired. He couldn't shovel—too much strain on his heart. But he could run the snowblower and watch it do all the work.

Near the shore the water had frozen into smooth glare ice. He knew this because he had been down checking on the ice every day. He had decided the town skating rink would be his project this year. But now the ice was covered with about a half a foot of snow. It would be a pleasure to clear it off—like watching his wife iron a tablecloth smooth of any wrinkles.

Sven stopped the truck close to the lake, walked around the back, dropped the tailgate, and pulled out his ramp. Then he climbed up into the truck and carefully pushed his snowblower down.

The wind was picking up across the lake. If it started blowing this snow around, he could be at this job all day long.

He could make out the shoveled outlines of the rink from when he had done it before. Pushing the snowblower in front of him, he aimed it at the far western corner. He'd start there and blow all the snow out of the rink. It took some strategy not to make this too much work.

Starting up the machine, he felt tired suddenly. He hadn't slept at all well last night. The face of that young girl, Stephanie, kept coming to him. She could be such a nice girl when she wanted to be. There was a rough side to her sometimes too—he knew she went drinking at the local bars and hung out with a tougher crowd—but she had always been real nice to him.

He had done a couple of rows when he stopped to take a breather. The sun was just glinting through the skim-milk-colored sky. Getting close to the shortest day of the year. Boy, he'd be glad when they got over that hump. He didn't mind cold, and he liked the snow, but he hated the darkness. It seemed to make it harder to get up everyday and easier to climb into bed on the early side.

He was getting ready to start the snowblower again when he heard a car coming down into the park. He turned to see, and recognized the car right away—the deputy sheriff's car.

He walked up the shore to greet her. Maybe she had news on Stephanie. She stopped the car next to his truck and rolled down her window.

"What do you know, Mrs. Watkins?"

"Sven, you've picked a cold one."

"I didn't pick it. You can't let the weather stop you from doing things. I've lived through many a winter, and you gotta keep moving."

"That is the secret, isn't it? Keep moving." Claire looked professional today, dressed in her uniform. "I wanted to give you the news on Stephanie and ask you a few more questions. Could I offer you a seat in my car? It's all warmed up."

"Sounds good. I figure I've got another hour out here, getting the rink cleared."

He walked around the car and pulled the passenger door open. The warmth of the car made his cheeks feel like they were burned.

"I'm sure glad you're doing the rink. My daughter is very excited about skating this year."

"I've seen her out here. She sure is persistent."

"Oh, that's the word for my Meg. Persistent."

"I worry about that spring on the other side of the park. It weakens the ice. Someone's going to go through if they're not careful. You tell Meg to stay away from there."

He pushed back the seat on the passenger side of the car so he had a little more leg room. Claire pushed back her seat too. "Wish I had some coffee to offer you," she said.

"Don't mind about that. Tell me how Stephanie is doing."

"She has regained consciousness, but I don't think she's doing much talking. The doctor I spoke with thinks she'll need some surgery for her nose and maybe her eyes."

"Jeez. That poor girl."

"Yeah. Now I wanted to ask when you got the call and when you got there."

"I listened to my machine again last night. Stephanie called me while I was at a friend's eating dinner. She left a message. I got there about five-forty-five. So somewhere in between."

"That jibes with what my sister said. She saw Stephanie stuck just before she got to my house. That gives us a three-hour window. I need to find out if anyone saw the car parked alongside the road."

"I wish I would have seen that guy." Sven had thought about what he could do with a shovel. His doctor told him to take it easy, but it would have been a pleasure to give that guy a licking.

"From a distance, Sven. We'll get him."

"I think they're linked." Claire told the sheriff. "At first, I suspected that Buck had been beating up Stephanie, even though everyone assured us he was gentle as a lamb. But now it's obvious that he wasn't the man."

"So who is?"

"I have work to do."

"Do it. I want this figured out before the poor woman gets out of the hospital."

Claire didn't tell him that might give her plenty of time. Stephanie's prognosis was not great. From the way the doctors were talking, she wouldn't be out for quite a while. "I'm on it."

Claire went into the computer and pulled all the information she could on Stephanie. She found Stephanie had parents in Eau Claire and a brother down in Winona, as Sandy the postmaster had thought. And then she found that she had been married once about five years ago, to a man named Tom Jackson. They hadn't been married long, and he lived in Eau Claire, which was only about fifty miles away.

Claire tried the parents first, the Klauses. A man answered the phone. "Is this Mr. Klaus?"

"Yeah. Whadda you want?"

Claire explained who she was and then said, "I'm calling about your daughter, Stephanie."

"She in trouble?"

"She was badly beaten up yesterday."

"How bad?"

"She's in the hospital, probably having surgery on her face right now."

"What do you want me to do?"

Claire was rather nonplussed. "Well, I'd like to know if you have any idea who could have done this to Stephanie. We found her badly beaten and don't know who did it to her."

"Stephanie doesn't really keep in touch with us. We haven't hardly known where she is for the last few years. She probably had it coming."

This man showed none of the normal parental reactions to a daughter being hurt. This was more than the stoical Scandinavian type that Claire ran into in Wisconsin. His lack of reaction went far beyond that. "Do you know her ex-husband?"

"Not really. We weren't invited to the wedding. I don't know that they even had one. Didn't last long. My wife could tell you more. She's sleeping at the moment. Late night. She works nights."

Claire gave up. She was going to get little from this man. "I'll try back later."

Claire thought of calling the ex-husband, but then decided it might suit her better to drive up and see him in person.

14

S HE was swathed in something. She couldn't tell what it was. She could feel it with her hands—if only she could lift them up that high. He was keeping her hostage. He had her locked up in a cellar. She couldn't see. She couldn't open her eyes. Her head throbbed; her face ached. She hurt in every cell of her body.

There was only one thing to do, one thing that would express the outrage of what she was feeling. She screamed as loud and long as she could. Maybe if she screamed long enough she would die. She wanted to die.

Suddenly there were hands on her arms. Someone, a woman, was talking to her. "It's okay. You're in the hospital. You were just in surgery. You're doing fine."

Stephanie couldn't remember what had happened. She was running away. Why couldn't she see? Why was she in the hospital? She had the car packed, the dog . . . Where was the dog? Had she left the dog to freeze in the snow?

She screamed again.

The woman took her hand. "You have to stop that. You

are disturbing everyone around you. Tell me what's the matter."

"My dog?"

There was silence. Then the woman said, "I'm sure he's fine. No one said anything had happened to the dog."

"My eyes?"

"You'll be okay. We've got them bandaged for now. The doctor will be in soon, and he'll take off the bandages."

"I hurt."

"Yes, I'm sure you do. We have you on Demerol. I'll give you a little more now. It should make you feel better."

She hoped this was no new trick of his. A woman to pretend she was a nurse. The dog had to be all right. He was such a good dog. She felt tears in her eyes, but where would the tears go? Her head hurt to its core. It rang like a bell. She thought, he hit me and hit me. Then a river flowed into her veins, and she floated away for a while.

When she came to consciousness again, a man was talking to her. He touched her arm, shook it gently, and said her name.

"What?" The word came out like a croak.

"Stephanie, I'm your doctor. Dr. Klein. How are you feeling?"

"Shit."

"I'm afraid that's to be expected. You've taken a pretty bad beating. We did some surgery on you this morning. Reset your nose and repaired your eyes. All of that will make you feel pretty lousy. But within a day or two, you should be feeling much better. Do you have any questions?"

"My dog?"

Again there was silence. "I'm not sure about your dog. The deputy might know. She's called a couple times and said she'd be down shortly."

"Watkins?"

"I believe that's her name."

Stephanie relaxed a little. If the woman had found her,

she would take care of Snooper. She was a good mother. She would know what to do. Then Stephanie remembered she needed to get away. If he did this to her, he would come again. She didn't even know if she was safe in the hospital.

"Stephanie, I want to take off the bandages over your eyes now that you're awake. You can tell me what you can see. We've got the lights very dim in the room, so it won't be a shock."

She could feel him unpeeling the tape from her face. She wanted to make him stop. Every little movement made her head ring and clang. It hurt so much she sucked in her breath.

"I'm being very gentle. Only a little more to go here," he said, and then, "There you go."

Stephanie opened her eyes. This time she saw some vague light and a white face close to hers. "Can you see me?"

"Yes," she said.

"What do I look like?"

"A blob of white."

"That's a start. How many fingers?" The face disappeared, and two sausages appeared in front of her face.

"Two."

"That's right. Encouraging. Let's turn up the lights a bit. Now, Stephanie, I'm going to slightly crank up your bed so you can look around." The back of the bed pushed into her from behind, forcing her to sit up. "Tell me what you can see."

Stephanie closed her eyes. She wasn't sure she wanted to see any more of the world. It was too hard. But then she knew she had to find out about her dog. She opened her eyes and looked as hard as she could. "The door," she said. It was darker over there. "The windows." A square of light shone in the room.

"Are you seeing as well as you normally do?"

"No, it's hard."

"I think you're doing well. Let's rest the eyes again for a while and try a little bit later."

Time drifted by her as the nurse came and gave her another bump of Demerol. Then someone new walked into the room. A clapping footstep sound.

The person stood next to her bed and sighed. Stephanie managed to open her eyes. She saw a woman with dark hair. Then she could make out the uniform.

"Where's my dog?" she asked.

"He's fine."

Tears came, and this time she felt them run down her cheeks. "He's fine?" she repeated.

"Yes, he's staying with a friend of mine. I think you know him—Rich Haggard. Snooper was guarding you when we got there."

"He was guarding me?"

"Sitting on top of you and growling."

"He's a good dog."

"He's a very good dog," Watkins agreed with her, then continued, "How're you feeling?"

Stephanie thought it was a stupid question. "Look at me. I feel like I look."

"I'm sorry."

The deputy's concern surprised Stephanie. "Thanks."

"Stephanie, I have to ask you some questions. You need to help me out here. Someone came over to your house yesterday and beat you very badly. They used a champagne bottle to do it."

"I don't remember anything at all. It's gone from my head," Stephanie said, which was the truth.

"I know this is hard. But I don't want this to happen to you ever again. Do you know who did it?"

She could guess. He had beat her so many times before, though never so badly she had to go to the hospital. But she couldn't tell. She had to get away. If she told, they would make her stay and fight him. She couldn't do it. They didn't know what he was like. He would win in the end.

"I don't know," she whispered.

Deputy Watkins stayed silent.

"I don't know who did it," Stephanie said a little louder.

Deputy Watkins sighed. "I was hoping you would remember and tell us so we could arrest him and protect you."

"I can't."

A nurse walked in the room and stood behind the deputy. "Stephanie, your brother called. He asked how you were doing. He said he'd try to stop by later and see you. He told me to tell you."

Stephanie nodded. Her brother checking on her.

"I'll be back to see if you've remembered anything. If you do, tell one of the nurses. They have my number. They'll call me, and I'll come right down."

Stephanie nodded again, just wanting the deputy to leave. She was too tired to do anything to save herself.

"You can't even guess who hurt you?" The deputy wouldn't give up.

Stephanie felt her head hurt from all the questions. "Not a clue," she said. The lies came so easily—she'd had a lifetime of practice.

Driving into Eau Claire, Claire realized it had been a while since she had come here. When Claire first moved to tiny Fort St. Antoine, she missed the big cities, but now she found them exhausting, the traffic more frustrating than ever.

She didn't know her way around Eau Claire very well, so she stopped, got out a good map, and located the street that Tom Jackson lived on.

Fifteen minutes later she parked in front of Jackson's house. She knocked on the door and waited, then knocked again. Finally a woman came to the door. Tall and thin, she looked unhealthy. Her hair was dull brown and oily, and her eyes looked like dark pools.

"What can I do for you?" she asked sullenly.

Claire was surprised the uniform didn't impress the woman a little more. Maybe she had seen it too many times. She decided to show her the badge too. "I'm here to talk to Tom Jackson . . . your husband?"

"He's not exactly my husband. Technically we're not married."

"Is he here?"

"Naw, he's at work. They had to work today. You should know that. Plus he gets time and a half."

"Who am I speaking with?"

"My name's Debby. Debby Thompson."

"Debby, may I come in?"

"You wanta come in? The house is a mess. Didn't clean up from last night." Debby backed up and let her into the living room. A crocheted afghan was piled on the couch. A pillow leaned against one arm of the couch. The woman had evidently been lying there when Claire came to the door.

Claire could see through to the dining room, where the table was covered with dirty dishes; empty bowls of food littered the middle, with the scrawny carcass of a turkey presiding over the whole mess.

Debby explained, "Had the parents over last night. I had made the whole meal and nobody offered to help with dishes, so I let them set."

"Was Tom with you all of yesterday?"

"Sure. Why? What's this about? Tom's okay, isn't he?"

"I'm not here to give you bad news about Tom. I'm here about someone else." Claire decided to try a different tack. "Did you know his ex-wife, Stephanie Klaus?"

"Heard about her. That's about all. Never met the woman. Tom doesn't have too much good to say about her. I'm just glad they didn't have any kids. Always makes it messier, hard on the kids. I've got three of my own. They're off at their grandparents' today." Debby put her hand to her head.

"Are you okay?"

"Oh, I get these migraines. I can't do nothing. Can't move. Can't stand noise or light. Just got to stick it out. I take pills, but they don't do much. You ever had a migraine?"

"No."

"Don't know how lucky you are." Debby sat down on the couch.

"So Tom didn't leave the house all day?"

"He left once. To go get some beer for dinner."

"What time was that?"

"Midafternoon."

"How long was he gone?"

"Didn't pay much attention. An hour or two."

"An hour or two? To get beer?" Claire questioned.

"He might have stopped for a few on the way."

The drive from Fort St. Antoine was about an hour. It might be possible.

"Where does Tom work?"

"You don't know?"

"No. Should I?"

The woman pulled the afghan over her shoulders and gave Claire the address of the Eau Claire police department. Claire felt like an idiot that she hadn't known he was a cop. He must have joined the force after he divorced Stephanie.

Claire had one more question. How do you ask a woman if her boyfriend is beating her? "Debby, how does he treat you?"

Debby looked at her oddly and then asked, "What do you mean?"

"Does Tom ever get rough with you?"

"What the hell is this about? It's none of your business. He's way better than a lot of the men I've known. He treats me fine."

Claire noticed that Debby hadn't said that Tom never hit her.

When Claire left the house, she thought of putting off the

talk with Tom Jackson until after she had checked him out through the grapevine. She didn't like to walk into interviews cold. But she didn't relish another drive to Eau Claire, especially if the weather stayed nasty. The roads were still icy from the last snowstorm, and they were talking about more on the way.

The police department was downtown in the old courthouse building. Claire loved the stonework of the building from the 1800s.

Tom Jackson stepped around his desk when he heard Claire call his name. He was a big man with a barrel chest and sandy hair. His eyes were dirty brown, and he had freckles like constellations on his face. He greeted her with a careful smile.

Claire flipped her ID for him. "Mr. Jackson, I'm here to ask you some questions about Stephanie Klaus."

He stepped back, shaking his head a little. "Stephanie Klaus, haven't thought of her in a while. What do you want to know? She all right?"

"You were married to her?"

"You must know that. What'd she say about me?"

"Stephanie didn't say anything."

"You been talking to Debby."

"I checked my contacts to find out where you were working."

"Yeah, I know a couple of guys work for Pepin County." He ran his eyes up and down her body. "Heard they had a good-looking woman working there. What do you want to know?"

"Have you seen Stephanie recently?"

"Haven't seen her in about four years, I think. No, I did run into her in Eau Claire once, but that was still a few years ago. I think she was visiting her folks. What's this about?"

"She was assaulted yesterday afternoon. She's in the hospital."

"How bad?"

She watched his eyes as she told him about Stephanie. "Broken nose, damage to her eyes."

He winced. "Jeez. She was a nice kid. Just didn't work out between us."

"May I ask why not?"

"Who's to say? We were too young, for starters. She was nineteen, I was twenty. I think she married me just to get out of the house. She didn't get along with her folks that good. I married her because it seemed the thing to do. She wanted it so bad. Then six months later, out of the blue, she left me. Never really knew why. Didn't care that much. I could tell it wasn't working out."

"Were you at home all yesterday?"

He bulked up right in front of her, chest out, arms crossed. "Don't tell me you think I had something to do with Stephanie. You gotta be kiddin'. I don't have to take this. Ask anyone around here what kind of cop I am. You have a lot of nerve coming in here and asking me questions."

Claire waited a few moments for him to calm down. "I'm sorry to offend you with my questioning. I'm just doing my job. You were home all yesterday?"

"Sure I was. It was Thanksgiving. Girlfriend cooked a nice meal. Her parents came over. That's all I did."

"Do you know anyone who might have done this to Stephanie?"

"I told you, I didn't really know her, and I certainly haven't had anything to do with her recently. I'd nearly forgotten all about her. But you might want to talk to her father. As I recall, he was a mean son of a bitch. They live right out of town."

Claire thought that might be a good idea.

Her brooch had gone missing. Mrs. Tabor had looked high and low for it. She had wanted to wear it on her dark burgundy wool dress for Thanksgiving at her daughter's. Her

husband had given her that brooch for their first wedding an-
niversary. She remembered he had told her that the past year
had been the best of his life, and he wanted a few more. They
had had many more together—nearly fifty before he had died
of a heart attack.

The brooch was a circlet of garnets. She knew they
weren't that expensive, not like rubies or anything, but she
loved the dark red color of them. The whole cluster had always looked so rich. She loved to wear her brooch, but she
saved it for special occasions. She didn't have much fancy
jewelry—a plain gold band served as her wedding ring—but
the brooch had always been her favorite piece. She usually
left it sitting on the top of her bureau.

She couldn't remember the last time she had seen it.
Thank goodness her daughter hadn't noticed she wasn't wearing it. Too much on her mind, with the big dinner and all. My,
it had been good. So nice to spend some time with her grandchildren. A happy family they were. They drove her home last
night, and she didn't get in bed until almost eleven. A very
late night for her.

But she hadn't slept well. She was fussed about the
brooch.

The worst of it was, she suspected Lily. She knew Lily had
liked that brooch. She had commented on it once or twice.
But she certainly couldn't come out and ask Lily if she took it.

She couldn't stand the thought that her brooch was gone
for good. She didn't have much left of her life with her husband, but that was one object she didn't want to let go of. She
had decided she would be buried with it. Seemed a little silly
to bury a good piece of jewelry, but she felt that no one would
ever feel about that little garnet circlet the way she did.

Plus women just didn't wear jewelry like that anymore.
Her granddaughters were very busy trying to be cool. One had
an earring in her nose, and the other had little silver balls lin-
ing her ear rim. They wouldn't be interested in a fussy
brooch.

She might be an old woman, but she was aware of the world around her.

When he gave her the brooch, her husband had told her that the circle represented his love for her, always true, never to be broken.

She wanted it back.

15

THE Klauses' mobile home squatted in a grove of trees just a few miles outside Eau Claire. Bales of hay encircled the skirting. Tires held down the roof. Claire thought that the trailer itself could have used some duct tape. The siding was falling off, and the roof over the entryway listed badly.

The sidewalk hadn't been shoveled. She kicked through snow up to the door and knocked. A strange scraping noise came from inside the trailer, and then the door burst open as if it had been released from a bungee cord.

An old man with a wild shock of white hair stared up at her from a wheelchair. "What do you want?" he asked. He ran a hand through his hair, and it stood up more wildly.

"Hello, Mr. Klaus. We spoke on the phone." She showed him her ID card. "May I come in?"

"I suppose. Sally's sleeping. She worked late last night."

Claire kicked her boots on the stairs to knock off the snow before she stepped into the trailer.

"I'd like to ask you some questions about Stephanie."

"How's she doing?"

"Better, I think." She was glad to see him show some meager interest in his daughter.

He backed up his wheelchair to give her room to come farther in, and she recognized the sound that she had been hearing as she stood outside. The trailer had so much furniture in it that his wheelchair scraped against chairs and the couch as he wheeled around. She sat down on the couch. The coffee table was covered with plates left from a variety of meals. Old orange peels and crusts of bread were strewn over the plates.

"As I told you, someone beat her up pretty badly yesterday. Whoever it was went after her with a glass bottle."

The old man shook in his chair. "Sounds bad."

"I talked to Stephanie in the hospital and asked her if she knew who had done it, but she says she can't remember. I wondered if you had any ideas about who might be responsible."

"At least you can't blame it on me," Mr. Klaus said and then laughed a laugh that turned into a cough. When he was finished hacking, he added, "I may have lifted my hand to that girl when she was a kid, but I couldn't do it anymore."

Claire looked at the old man and wondered if he wasn't ultimately responsible for Stephanie's predicament, teaching her that she should expect to get beaten. What a lesson to give a daughter.

"Anyone from her past?"

"Stephanie didn't have many boyfriends. She was pretty enough, but I was kinda strict with her. Until she run off and got married. They weren't married long. Have you thought about him? I forget his name."

"Yes, sir. I've talked to him."

"Big guy. I think he's a cop now."

"Anyone else?"

"Harry?" A woman's voice came from the back of the trailer. "Who've you got out there?"

"A cop. Asking about Stephanie. I told you she got hurt."

A woman walked out of the back room, buttoning up a sweater. She was in her late fifties and had even lighter blond hair than Stephanie's, short and done in a frizzy shag. "No, you did not. You didn't tell me anything. What's going on with Stephanie?" The woman turned and addressed the question to Claire.

"She was assaulted and spent the night in ICU."

"My baby. How bad is she?" Mrs. Klaus opened a pack of cigarettes, tapped out one, turned on the gas burner, and lit it from the flame.

"I talked to her today. Her eyesight isn't good, and she had to have her nose reset, but she's doing better than they expected."

"Who did it?" the woman spit out.

"She doesn't seem to know."

"She's lying. She knows."

"Why are you so sure?"

Mrs. Klaus blew out a puff of smoke. "I know her. She keeps everything to herself. Just her way. She'd get beat up when she was living with us and not tell me a thing."

"A boyfriend?"

"She didn't seem to have any. She claimed she was clumsy. I didn't push it."

Claire wondered if the abuser had been Mr. Klaus. "What about her ex-husband?"

"I'd be surprised. He's a cop, after all. Plus I don't think they've stayed in touch over the years."

"Anyone else I could talk to?"

"Have you tried Johnny, our son?"

"No—would he know something?"

"Maybe. He and Stephanie have been pretty close in the past. Then they had a falling-out. But I bet he might know something."

Claire told them the name of the hospital where Stephanie was being treated and then stood up to leave.

Mrs. Klaus stubbed out her cigarette in an old orange

peel that was sitting on the table. "Harry was pretty bad with his hands when he could still get around. He gave me a black eye or two and was always taking after the kids. I would have left him if he hadn't been so sick. He's got MS. He's lucky to have me now, aren't you, Daddy?"

The old man scowled at her.

Scott decided that if Claire got back to work in time, he was definitely going to ask her to go have a drink with him and Billy. It was Friday night. They didn't do it every night, but they had a standing date to get a beer or two on Friday nights. Claire hadn't been included in much of the socializing with the other deputies. Stan, Fremont, and some of the older guys didn't care for her. Thought she had moved in on their territory. But Scott admired her. Maybe it had taken him a while to warm up to her, but she did her work. You had to give her that. Billy liked her too.

At five to five, she came in the door. He stood up, walked over to her desk, and sat down in her chair.

She walked up to him, tapped him gently on the shoulder, and said, "What's up, Scotty?"

"You're in a good mood."

"I decided to be. I've got a plan."

"How about you going out for a drink with Billy and me? We're heading out in a few minutes."

"A drink? God, that sounds like a good idea. Okay. How 'bout Shirley's? That way I can talk to the bartender who was on the night that Owens was killed. I think he's working tonight."

"You got it. We'll meet you there."

They all three drove separately. Scott reached Shirley's first. He grabbed a booth, saving it with his coat and walking up to the bar just as Claire and Billy came in. "The first one's on me," he said.

"Let me get it," Claire insisted. "It will be the only one for me. I've gotta get home to my daughter."

They all ordered Leinenkugel on tap and sat at the booth Scott had claimed. The bar was filling up fast. They clinked their glasses together and drank.

After another sip, Claire asked, "You guys know a cop named Tom Jackson, works up in Eau Claire?"

Billy nodded his head. "I think I know him. Big blond guy?"

"Yeah, that sounds right. You hear how he is as a cop?"

"He was a year ahead of me at the academy. People left him alone. Not so much that he had a temper, but he was unpredictable."

"Like how?"

"You couldn't joke with him. He didn't get it. Very serious. That's all I remember."

"You heard anything about him, Scott?"

"No, but I know someone on the Eau Claire force. Should I ask around?"

"Please do. He was married to Stephanie Klaus a few years ago. I think he needs to be checked out."

Scott remembered the brutal scene at Stephanie Klaus's place. The ambulance had taken the woman away by the time he got there, but there was still blood everywhere. He understood Claire's urgency.

Billy said, "I don't like the idea of looking at a cop."

Scott remembered his dad slapping his mom around when he was a kid. She had divorced him and taken Scott and his brother to live on the farm with his grandparents. "I'll check him out for you, Claire."

Claire smiled at him. She must have put lipstick on in her car before she came to the bar, and she'd let her hair down. Scott was going to see his girlfriend Cindy later on. They were going out to eat at the Fish House. He liked Cindy, but couldn't see himself hooking up with her permanent. He was having fun just hanging out. But when Claire smiled at him, something buzzed inside him that never did when Cindy gave him a sexy look, and Claire wasn't even trying.

He knew that Claire was seeing someone. Rich Haggard—nice older guy, pretty quiet. Scott wasn't about to move in on Claire; it was a bad idea to be seeing someone you work with, anyway, probably against the rules. But he sure liked having her around work. She made him feel like there were places a woman could take him that he hadn't been yet. He was determined to get there with someone. Hell, who knows? Maybe she and Rich would break up. Anything could happen. He knew Claire was in her early forties. He was going to be thirty-five. Seven or eight years wasn't too much of a stretch. She looked young enough.

"Another beer?" he asked Billy.

"Let me go up with you," Claire said, grabbing his arm. "I want to talk to the bartender. That's the one, isn't it?" She pointed at a stocky dark-haired man with glasses. He was laughing at a customer's joke.

"Yeah, that's who I talked to that night."

"Stay with me. You know what he said that night."

Claire got the bartender's attention. Scott had reminded her of the guy's name. "Norm, I know you're busy here, but could you give me a minute or two to talk about what happened the night Buck Owens died?"

"I'll do my best."

"How did Owens seem to you that night?"

"What, now I'm a shrink? Same as always. He was a pretty easygoing guy."

"Do you remember anything in particular about him when he came in?"

"Actually, I do. He came in the door, and his glasses fogged up. He walked up to the counter and set them down in front of me. He ordered a beer. I remember thinking that I couldn't tell whether his eyes were tearing from the cold or he was crying. That's what I thought. I handed him his glasses, and he took his beer. He was fine."

"You touched his glasses?"

"Yeah. A law against that?"

"No, but we'd like to get your prints. Can you come by the sheriff's department?"

"I'll swing by tomorrow."

"Was he with anyone?"

"Not that I noticed. We weren't terribly busy that night."

"Was anyone in here that you didn't know?"

The man wrinkled up his face. He was trying to please, but didn't have much to offer. Scott hadn't gotten much more out of him that night. "Hard to remember, but I don't recall anyone."

"Did you notice when he left?"

"Now, that's what was funny. I didn't notice that. But then I saw the dog sitting in the middle of the floor, staring at the door. I looked around for Buck, and figured he stepped out for a second. He wouldn't forget his dog."

Claire perched on a stool for a moment and swung around to face Scott. "I better head home. I'm really glad you asked me to have a drink."

"Long overdue."

The truck slipped on the road, then found the gravel and lurched forward. Rich looked down at the little dog snuggled next to his leg as he headed the truck up the hill to Claire's house. "I'm glad to have you along, little buddy. We're going to a house full of women—four of them to be exact—and another male presence will be welcome. You stick by me."

When he walked in the door, Snooper became the center of attention. Meg immediately knelt in front of him and offered him Rachel's rattle.

"Not a good idea. Rachel's too young to share with a dog,"

Claire said and then reached down to pet the small dog's head.

Bridget swooped the dog up, and he licked her face over and over again.

Rich stood and watched all the attention they were showering on Snooper.

Finally Meg noticed him. She leaned her head against Rich's leg. "I like the dog. I wish we could keep him."

Claire walked over and gave him a peck.

Bridget said, "Hello, Rich. Claire's getting looped tonight. She went out with the boys after work."

Claire laughed and walked into the kitchen. He followed her, leaving everyone else cooing over Snooper. Then he took her in his arms and gave her a real kiss. She smelled warm and tasted sweet with beer. She kissed him back with just enough warmth to make him feel welcome.

When he had called her earlier at work and asked to come over, she had sounded hesitant. He knew she didn't want him to come because her sister was going to be there, but he had gently argued her out of her concern, saying, Bridget certainly knows what we're doing.

He managed to keep himself from complaining that they hadn't been together in five days. He would only admit to himself that he needed the feel of her body next to his in the night.

This is what he hated about love, the need of it.

16

"M RS. Watkins, I need to talk to you about your daughter." Mr. Turner's eyebrows flew across his forehead. Although only in his thirties, he had eyebrows that were starting to sprout auxiliary hairs, and he moved them with great effect when he was excited.

Claire found herself cranking her head back to look up at the man as he loomed over her. She realized this whole conference thing was set up to intimidate the parent. Here she was sitting in a kid's desk that was too small for her, and he was standing up in front of her. Why hadn't they met in a nice comfortable lounge? It made her feel like she was trapped back in school.

Suddenly, she had great sympathy for her daughter and wondered if she shouldn't consider home-schooling. And the teacher hadn't even started the lecture. She just knew it was coming.

She replied, "That is the purpose of this meeting, isn't it?"

"You have a very smart daughter."

Flattery. Another bad sign. "She is, isn't she? Don't know how it happened. Her father, I guess."

"But—"

Claire knew it had been coming—"the big But," as Meg called it. "Yes?"

"But she is working way below her potential."

Claire decided it was time to make a suggestion. "We had considered having her skip fifth grade. Maybe we should reconsider that?"

This shook him, she could tell. "Well, I think that might not be what's called for under these circumstances."

"Tell me about the circumstances," Claire crossed her ankles and put her hands in her lap. She knew how to be a good student.

"She doesn't seem to be able to focus on the task at hand. She only wants to read in class and doesn't want to attend to her schoolwork. She has been behind on getting several assignments in, which leads me to believe that she is not faithfully doing her homework." Then he gave her the evil eye. "Mrs. Watkins, do you check in with your daughter about her homework every night?"

Claire almost laughed. She had never had to check on Meg, her perfect child, who sometimes seemed independent. "No, it's never been necessary with Meg before. She's very self-motivated."

"Well, children change. Meg seems to be going through a stubborn period. She doesn't want to do things the way I want them done. I fear we're having a test of wills. And I will win it, Mrs. Watkins, I will."

He was a bully. It was as simple as that, or as complicated. Poor, dear Meg. It would do little good for Claire to antagonize him, much as she wanted to. He seemed to dislike her on the spot, maybe because she was Meg's mother or maybe because she was a working woman, possibly even because she was a cop. Claire didn't even care to try to figure it out. She was here to help her daughter.

"What do you suggest we do, Mr. Turner?" She looked up at him and gave him her winningest smile.

"Well, I am encouraged to find you so agreeable to listen to my slight complaints about your daughter's behavior."

"Meg will certainly hear about this when I get home."

"If you could stress to her how important it is to follow the rules. Teaching a group of twenty-five children can only be done when there is law and order." He allowed himself a crooked smile, alluding as he had to her job as deputy. "I'm sure you understand."

The man thought he was amusing, Claire thought. But onward. "Meg can be a free thinker. I will talk to her about all this."

"I think if she understands that her mother is behind me, I will be able to get someplace with her."

A sadistic bully. She forgot that teaching could be an ideal job for them and that country schools without easy access to good teaching stock might need to hire them just to fill the classrooms. Get someplace with her, indeed.

Claire stood. She couldn't take this sitting down anymore. Mr. Turner wasn't much taller than her, so they almost saw eye to eye. "How are Meg's grades?"

He backed up to his desk and sat on the edge of it. "They're in the B range."

"So she's not making a complete mess of it?"

His eyes bugged slightly, and his eyebrows were flying circles above them. "No, not at all. But we both know she can do so much better. All she seems to want to do is read books."

"Not exactly a horrible problem, is it?" Claire asked.

"No," he admitted. "But if all the other children are working and one is reading, that can be disruptive."

"Reading?"

Mr. Turner nodded.

Claire thought for a moment. "Well, Mr. Turner. I was thinking that we should have a carrot to dangle in front of the donkey, and I suggest that if my daughter behaves and gets her work done, I will tell her you have given her permission to read as long as she is very quiet about it."

She had him.

"Well, all right."

She reached out and shook his hand. "So nice to meet you. I'm glad we had this talk."

He sat down on the edge of his desk and looked relieved as she walked out of the room. She resisted adding, "Class dismissed."

Stephanie woke up in real pain. They had been easing her off the Demerol. She was no longer on the drip. They had awakened her once in the night to give her pain pills, but that was four hours ago. Stephanie knew it was four hours ago because that's how long the pills lasted. And then she woke up. And wanted to scream, but she resisted doing that again.

She buzzed the nurse and waited, counting the moments until she came. Stephanie knew she was getting better because even though the pain was bad, it was tolerable. It felt real because it wasn't over the top anymore. At first it had felt as if the top of her head was going to lift off with the agony of it all.

They had had her sitting up in a chair yesterday, but today she was supposed to walk down the hall. They promised her catheter would come out and she would be completely mobile.

Her sight was returning nicely, the doctors said. Someone came in about twice a day and shone a little tiny flashlight into her eyes. They had set up an eye chart on the far wall, and they would ask her what letters she was seeing. She had them memorized by now, but tried not to cheat.

Today, she would need to analyze how her body was doing and figure out when she could leave. She hoped in another day or two. They didn't seem to be in any hurry to let her out of the hospital, which was fine with her. She did feel safe in the hospital, always someone bustling around. She could stay here forever—except she missed Snooper.

Her brother thought she was going to go and stay with him, but she would not do that. Then there was the women's shelter in Durand. But they would never let her have the dog there.

She would leave before they thought she was ready. She would bolt. She had thought it all out.

Sven would come and get her. He had helped her out before. She needed to thank him anyway for coming to her rescue on Thanksgiving. Deputy Watkins said Sven had been quite upset when he found her. Stephanie couldn't remember a thing.

She would have him drive her right to Rich Haggard's and pick up Snooper. She would ask Sven to dig out her car before she got home. It was still all packed. The deputy said they hadn't touched anything. She was ready to go. She would put Snooper in the car and drive westward as long as she could, and then she would get a hotel room and sleep.

That was the plan.

There was another one.

She could tell Deputy Watkins what was going on. This plan had been growing stronger in her mind since Watkins had been in to see her. Points in her favor: she was a woman, she had taken care of the dog, and she promised that she would personally see that Stephanie was not hurt if she would just tell her who had beat her up. Stephanie believed her.

The only thing that worried her was that no one understood how hard Jack would fight to get at Stephanie. No one except herself.

It wasn't that she didn't trust the police this time, it was more that she didn't think they were up to the task.

And she had Snooper to think about.

✦

A few days after Mrs. Tabor had discovered her brooch was missing, Lily had come to work wearing it.

Mrs. Tabor couldn't believe her eyes. Lily had the beautiful garnet brooch, as plain as day, pinned to her chest.

Mrs. Tabor couldn't help herself. She had to say something. The words flew out of her mouth without her thinking about it. "Why are you wearing my brooch? I've been looking for that everywhere."

Lily gave her a look and laughed. "Oh, Mrs. Tabor. I told you you might forget. You gave it to me. It was such a nice gift."

The laugh was not a very nice laugh. Mrs. Tabor did not believe her. She would never, even if she had completely lost her mind, give her brooch away to anyone. And, of course, if it went to anyone, it would be her daughter. But Mrs. Tabor had planned on being buried with it pinned to her chest.

"I gave it to you?" she said back to Lily.

"Yes, don't you remember? I always told you how much I liked it. Then, for my birthday, you gave it to me. Took it off your dresser and handed it to me. I thought I'd wear it so you could see how much I appreciated your gift."

Mrs. Tabor felt as if her head was about to fall off. Would she do such a thing and then not remember it? How scary a land was this growing old—filled with land mines and booby traps. Not being able to trust your own memory. It was too much.

She had to get out of the room before she said something that she would regret. Truth be told, she was afraid of Lily.

"I don't think I want to go out today, Lily. If you don't mind going to the store for me, I think I'll just have a lie down."

"Sure thing, Mrs. Tabor. You look a little tuckered out. You didn't sleep good last night?"

"Sleep is very elusive when you're my age. Sometimes it wraps itself around you and won't let you go, and other times it runs away from you. Last night was one of the bad ones."

Mrs. Tabor went to the bedroom, stretched out on her bed, and pulled a thin blanket over her legs. A little nap. She crawled back under the covers only when she was sick. For a nap in the afternoon, she slept on top of the bed-clothes.

When she heard Lily leave the house, she pushed herself off the bed and went to the phone. She had marked the number in the phone book, and she punched it in carefully.

"Pepin County Sheriff's Department."

"Is Deputy Watkins there?" she asked the pleasant woman who had answered the phone.

"Hold a moment."

"Hello, Watkins here."

"You sound like a real deputy."

"I am. Who am I speaking with?"

"Sorry, this is Mrs. Tabor. Do you remember me?"

"Yes, of course. What can I do for you?"

"Well, she's at it again. That Lily. She can be nice when she wants to be, but I think she's got a bad side to her. First it was the checks, but I let it slide. That was a mistake. And now she's taken my brooch. Well, I've had enough of it."

There was silence on the other end. Maybe she had said too much.

"What would you like me to do?"

"Get back my brooch."

"How have you been, Claire?" Dr. Lynn Potter asked as she ushered Claire to a seat on a couch and took a chair close by.

Claire should have known she wouldn't get away without talking about herself even though she had made it clear when she called that it was a business meeting; she would be asking advice on a case. Claire had persuaded the sheriff to pop for the half-hour fee. "Basically fine."

"Covers a lot, doesn't it? Fine."

"I do a hard job. It stirs things up. But I feel like you

helped me figure out ways to cope better. Is that what you want to hear?"

There was a pause while Dr. Potter looked her over. Claire realized her answer had been a little sharp.

"What I want to hear? You called and asked to see me."

"Sorry. I'm having trouble with a case, as I explained to you on the phone. Abuse. A battered woman. I just don't get it. How can women let men do that to them? Grown-up women."

"Tell me about the case," Dr. Potter suggested. She leaned forward in her chair and tucked her brown bobbed hair behind her ears.

So Claire did. Without giving any names, she told the doctor about Stephanie, Buck, the dog. She told her about the phone call, the car-through-the-ice murder of Buck Owens, the last battering on Thanksgiving Day. She felt her heart race as she talked about it and tried to calm herself down.

"You sound pretty angry, Claire."

"She won't give me anything. She won't let me help her."

"That has to be very frustrating. But you need to come to understand her and have compassion for her situation before you are going to get her to talk to you. That's what I think."

"Makes sense. Can you help me with the compassion part?"

"I can't give it to you, but we can talk about it. Why don't you start by telling me what you don't understand?"

"Well, I've never let a man hit me and get away with it. Once, when I was at the academy, a guy I was dating grabbed me too hard and shook me. That was it. I was out of there!"

"Did you love him?"

"No."

"Did you want to marry him, live with him the rest of your life?"

"No."

"Makes it easier to walk away. One thing that might help

is to think of someone you love. Think of what you would do if they hit you. Think how hard it might be to give up all that is good between you and walk away."

"So like if Rich hit me?"

"Good, you're still seeing Rich."

"His mother came over for Thanksgiving."

"Great, how'd it go?"

"A bit of an ordeal, but at least we've met."

"So what would you do if he hit you?"

Claire tried to go there, but it seemed impossible. "He wouldn't do that. I'm with him because he wouldn't do that."

"What about your husband?"

Claire remembered Steve getting really mad. Once he had broken the dining room window. She couldn't even remember why he had been so mad. It had been just before Meg was born. Claire had been frightened, but as soon as he broke the window, he calmed down. He laughed. He apologized. What if he wouldn't have done that? She was pregnant. Would she have left her husband if he had slugged her? "I don't think I could have left right away. I would have warned him that I would leave if he ever did it again. I would have given him another chance."

"Fair enough. And then four months later, he hits you again. And he's sorry afterward, really sorry. Promises he'll never do it again."

"I don't know."

"It's hard to know unless it happens to you. I do think you're a pretty healthy woman and you have learned to walk away from what hurts you, but we all have our weaknesses."

"I suppose."

"What if you were in love with a man and he loved you, and in order to have you he killed someone? Would you turn him in? Would you let all the world see what kind of man he really was? Or would you protect him? Cover up for him? Because you loved him."

Claire sat still. She felt like she had been slugged in the

belly. She couldn't look at Dr. Potter. How could she have used that against her? How could she have pulled it out of the closet and stuck her with it?

"I know this is your job, but that hurt," Claire finally said.

"I bet. But maybe it will help you understand this woman better. We all have our weak areas, as I said before. You have yours. You have begun to forgive yourself. You have some compassion for yourself. Carry it over to this woman."

Claire sat and took in what Dr. Potter was saying. Dr. Potter uncrossed her legs and crossed them the other way. Claire was sure if you could read body language that this movement meant something. Then Dr. Potter asked, "What else is bothering you about this case?"

A feeling washed over Claire, strangely close to sorrow. She tried to describe it. "I feel so helpless. It's my job to help people, to protect them. Stephanie lives in my town. I know her. But she won't let me help her. I can't seem to protect her. We were eating turkey, and she was getting beaten to a pulp. It makes me sick."

"I bet. It should."

"What can I do?"

"Just feel it. Just know you're feeling it. It makes you a good deputy. You care about people."

Claire was surprised that Dr. Potter's words made her feel better. She hadn't told her anything she could do to get over the feeling, yet her words were still reassuring. "Can you tell me anything else that will help me reach her before it's too late?"

"I have worked with several abused women. It isn't exactly my area of expertise, but what I've learned is that they usually have something in their lives that they will fight for. It often isn't themselves. Often their children, sometimes friends, family. If you can find out what that is, you can get them to stand up for themselves. The other thing I've seen is that they do need to stand up for themselves. They might suffer immediately, but eventually it is the only way to end the abuse."

Claire thought about Stephanie and finding her lying in the snow in her driveway. One thing that had struck Claire was that the dog hadn't been hurt. The dog was so small and defenseless. What had Stephanie done so that the dog hadn't been hurt?

"I think the dog is the answer."

17

I T'S grown four inches in the last three days," Meg told her mother after carefully measuring the amaryllis plant.

The plant was shooting up a thick green stalk with a bud on the end. The stalk was as big around as two of her fingers put together. Meg was hoping that it would bloom on Christmas Eve. A present for everyone. That would be perfect. Every morning she checked it. Beatrice had told her only to water the amaryllis every few days, but not to let it go bone dry. "The nourishment comes from the bulb," Beatrice had told her.

"That is one amazing plant." Her mother was making oatmeal for the two of them. "I thought I'd drive you to school this morning."

Meg ran and got bowls and spoons and handed them to her mom. "Yay! That bus ride is too dang long."

"Where did you learn to say 'dang'?"

"Everyone on the school bus says even worse. Especially the boys. They swear all the time. The bus driver just ignores it."

"Well, you might want to follow suit." Claire dished out a big bowl of oatmeal and handed Meg the brown sugar in a plastic bowl. Meg's theory was, put enough brown sugar on anything and it was edible.

After three spoonfuls, her mother decided to put a stop to it. "Hey, leave some for me."

Meg handed back the brown sugar.

"We didn't get a chance to talk about my conference with your teacher last night. I thought we could talk about it today before school." Her mom handed her the milk in a small white pitcher. It was nice and cold from the refrigerator.

Meg made a face. She had worried about that dang conference last night before bed. It had even kept her up for a while. But she hadn't wanted to bring it up.

"What do you think of Mr. Turner, Meg?"

This had to be a trick question. "Truthfully?"

"Yes, you can say how you really feel to me."

"But I know I'm supposed to be respectful of my teachers."

"I'm glad you've learned that. And I don't want you to forget it, but people also have to earn your respect."

"I think he's a meanie," Meg told her.

"Why?"

Meg made a well in the middle of her oatmeal and poured in the milk. "Hey, I'm just a kid, and he likes to push me around. And I'm not the only one in class that he does it to. But I think he picks on me more because I'm smarter. I think that's one of the reasons he doesn't like me."

"I think you might be right. Do you think you are smarter than him?"

Meg looked at her mom to see if she could figure out what was the right answer to that question. Her mother's face was a blank. Meg decided to just say what she thought. If it got her in trouble, at least she would get her mother's honest reaction. "I'm not much dumber than him right now, and when I'm his age, I'm going to be a lot smarter than he is, that's for sure."

Her mother nodded. "I think you're right again. You are smart. Now let me ask you another question. I don't think you and Mr. Turner are getting along very well. Do you think there's anything you can do to change that?"

Meg was afraid of this. Now the lecture was coming. She said what she knew her mother would want her to say.

"Do what he says," she said reluctantly. Then she started to eat her oatmeal.

"Yes, you could do that. But I think you're smart enough to figure out a way so that Mr. Turner thinks he's getting what he wants, but you also get what you want. I think you need to work on this problem. You've had nice teachers up till now, and I'm glad. But there are a lot of Mr. Turners in this world. I don't like him very much, but he is your teacher. I'd like to see you try to win this battle with Mr. Turner without getting into more trouble. To do that, you need to make Mr. Turner think that he has won."

"Wow, Mom. That's really complicated."

"Do you think you could try?"

"Sure, I can try." She was nearly finished with her oatmeal. Mom would drive her to school. Everything was possible. "It might be kinda fun."

"That's my girl. I did ask Mr. Turner to let you read in class if you got all your work done. I think he's agreeable to that."

Meg looked up at her mom. She felt relieved that they had talked about Mr. Turner and her mother hadn't yelled at her. But there was something else that had been bothering her. She couldn't stop thinking about it. "The kids on the bus are saying that the woman who got beaten almost died. They said she doesn't have any face left. Is that true?"

Her mom picked up her bowl and brought it to the sink. Then she turned and leaned against the sink and said, "She was badly beaten, but she's doing pretty well. Her face is going to be fine. I would prefer you not talk to the kids about the work I'm doing."

"Oh, I know that, Mom. You already told me. But I can't help it if they talk about it to me?"

"I guess not."

"I'm worried about the little dog."

"You don't need to be, sweetie. You know Rich will take good care of him."

Then Meg brought up her real concern. "But what if that man comes to our house?"

"I know it's hard to understand, but that man is only after Stephanie. It's like he thinks he owns her, that he can do what he wants with her, but he can't."

"Are you going to stop him, Mom?"

"Yes, whatever it takes, I will stop him."

"Is Tom Jackson there?"

"Yeah, let me try his desk. I saw him walk into the office a few minutes ago. Give me a sec."

Billy had called the Eau Claire police department to give Tom Jackson a heads-up on the Stephanie Klaus case. He hadn't really told Watkins the complete truth the other night. He wasn't sure why, except that he wanted to hear what she had to say first before he revealed how well he knew Tom. Then when he heard what it was about, he decided he should keep quiet.

He and Jackson had been good buddies when they were at the academy. He had stuck pretty close to the truth. Jackson was ahead of him at the academy and was very serious. But Jackson had helped him out on assignments a number of times, and Billy felt like he owed him. This phone call would barely begin to pay him back.

Jackson came on the line. After exchanging greetings, Billy got right to the point. "A deputy from here is checking up on you for an assault case."

"Thanks for calling about that. She stopped by the other day. What was her name? Watson, Watkins? Man, she's a looker. I'd like to do mouth-to-mouth on that deputy sheriff any old day."

"Yeah, Watkins is all right." Billy never liked the cracks guys made about Claire. Some women played the babe part, but Claire never acted provocative in any way. She did her job straight on.

"She think I have anything to do with Stephanie?"

"We went out for a drink the other night. She really didn't say too much. Just was asking about you. Thought I'd let you know."

"Hey, I appreciate it. I'd like to be kept abreast of the situation."

"So you were married to this Stephanie Klaus? I don't think I even knew you'd been married. You've been staying in touch with her? Still friends?"

"Naw, not really. We were married before I was at the academy. After the divorce, we didn't have too much to do with each other. I still see her folks in town once in a while, but her dad never liked me that much. To tell you the truth, I'd pretty much forgot all about her. Until this Watkins showed up. So can you give me a good word with her?"

"Yeah, I'll do that."

"How is Stephanie doing?"

"I haven't seen her. Buddy of mine is working the case with Claire. From the sound of it, she got it pretty bad. Beat up with a champagne bottle. You got any idea who might have done this to her? Anyone from her past?"

"Haven't the foggiest. I don't think Stephanie liked champagne," Tom said and then chuckled as if he had made a joke.

"But I guess she's recovering pretty good. She's still in the hospital."

"What hospital?"

For a moment, Billy thought of not telling him. It was sort of confidential information. But Tom was a cop too. He might come up with something. "St. Catherine's, here in Durand."

"Listen, if you do see her, say hi to her from me, would you?"

As Claire drove through Fountain City, she saw the bank sign flash the temperature as zero degrees and the time as twelve-twenty. The day was clear and sunny. The coldest days were usually sunny, brittle in their brightness, the snow creaking beneath each footstep. The sky looked like an enameled blue bowl over the white cup of the bluffs.

As she left the town, she saw bald eagles sitting on the edge of the river ice where the water still ran open, waiting to scavenge dead, floating fish.

Claire had thought about calling John Klaus, but then realized that she needed to see him in person. He was Stephanie's older brother. He was a lawyer. He had been close to Stephanie. He might be Claire's way in to her. It was worth a try.

Before she had left for Winona, she had pulled the phone records on Buck Owens and Stephanie Klaus. Although local calls could not be retrieved, long distance calls were kept on record. John Klaus had called Stephanie several times in recent weeks. Not so unusual for siblings to do. But there had also been a call from Winona to Buck Owens. It had been made at a pay phone. Maybe it meant nothing, but she would ask about it.

She had almost nothing else to go on in his murder case. The crime lab had found nothing useful in the car. She felt like they were at a dead end. Claire kept coming back to the link she felt existed between Buck's death and Stephanie's beating. Maybe she would find it in Winona.

She drove over the river to cross into Minnesota and then located the main street of Winona. The small town, like most of the river towns, was being discovered. John Klaus was a real estate lawyer; if he was able to take advantage of the boom time, he was probably prospering.

His office was in a thirties-style bungalow, a one-story house built of dark brick. She walked in the front door, and the secretary took her name, staring at her uniform. Claire had called ahead for an appointment but hadn't explained the nature of the meeting. She wanted an element of surprise. She wanted to see how John Klaus behaved when he was caught off guard.

He walked out of his office and held out his hand to her. Even though he looked young, he seemed very confident, and not at all surprised to see Claire in her deputy's uniform. When Claire got her first look at him, she was surprised at what a handsome man he was. But while the resemblance to his father was striking, there was little similarity between him and Stephanie. John Klaus was around five-ten, but seemed taller as he stood ramrod-straight. He had thick, sandy hair cut short and was wearing a well-cut suit.

"I didn't realize you were a police officer," he admitted as they shook hands.

"Deputy sheriff," Claire corrected.

"Is this about Stephanie? I don't know if I can be of help to you." He didn't motion her into his office.

"Can we step into your office?" Claire suggested.

"Certainly." He waved her in.

The room had floor-to-ceiling built-in bookshelves on one wall. Various diplomas and certificates were hung on the opposite wall. His desk was in the front of a large, many-paned window that looked out onto the street.

He settled behind his desk, and she sat in one of the red leather chairs opposite it. "Your sister, Stephanie, was badly beaten several days ago."

"I'm aware of that. I've been to see her at the hospital."

"She says she doesn't know who beat her up. I'm not sure I believe her. I'm wondering if you could shed any light on this incident."

John Klaus sunk his face into his hands and then came out of them and looked at Claire. "I wish I could. I talked to her about that. She stonewalled me too. When I saw what that creep had done to her with a bottle of champagne, I couldn't believe it. I'm praying that she will recover her health and her looks. I don't know if you knew her from before, but Stephanie was a very pretty woman."

"Yes, she was." Claire remembered her smile. "Did you ask her what had happened?"

"Yes. But she wouldn't tell me who had done it. I tried to get it out of her."

"Can you guess who it might be?"

"Lately Stephanie and I haven't been as close as we once were. I married this last year, and she doesn't care for my wife. It's unfortunate. I fear she might be a little jealous. In fact, it's been months since I've seen her."

"Did you know Buck Owens, Stephanie's friend?"

"Never met the guy. Just heard about him from Stephanie. But wasn't he killed recently when his car went through the ice?"

"Yes. Stephanie's had a rough time lately. Sounds like your childhood wasn't that idyllic either. Did your father abuse you both?"

John Klaus stiffened. His easy manner disappeared, and his eyes shifted away from her face and out the window for a moment. When he spoke, Claire detected anger in his voice. "Our father did the best he could. He had a temper. No big deal."

"What about her ex-husband? Could he have come after Stephanie? Been jealous of Buck?"

"Now, that's a possibility. She did tell me that he could be very difficult sometimes."

"Has he seen her lately?"

"Not that I know of, but Stephanie probably wouldn't tell me if they were in touch. She knew I didn't approve of him. They married while I was in the service. When I came out, it was a done deal. But she came to regret it."

"Why? Why did they get divorced?"

John Klaus shrugged his shoulders. "Just not suited at all. Stephanie's a very sensitive woman. She was lucky to be rid of him."

Claire could hear the affection for Stephanie in his voice. "Is there anyone else you can think of that Stephanie might have confided in?"

"Not really. She was always kind of a loner. Kept to herself. We had each other when we were growing up, but then I left to join the Marines. She was on her own. I think that's why she got married. She never made women friends easily."

Claire had found that to be the case. She had called the women that worked with Stephanie at the W.A.G. factory and the women artists she had shared a booth with at the art fair. They all said she was nice, but quiet. Kept to herself. Seemed a little wary. Never picked up on their overtures to be friends.

John Klaus pushed his chair back and stood. Claire sat for a moment, trying to think of what else she could ask that would get her to understand Stephanie a little better.

"Why would she protect this man?" she asked him.

"Why are women the way they are."

18

THE next morning Stephanie woke without the pounding in her head. She stood up carefully, and the world didn't rush in on her. She shuffled to the bathroom and peed and washed her face and hands. The warm water on her face felt good. Then she did the bravest act of all—she looked in the mirror.

She had learned that she always looked the worst about four days after the beating. What a thing to know. And sure enough, she looked like some kind of nightmare creature. The purple around her eyes had turned nearly black in its bruising. Her eyes were still bloodshot. Her nose was disformed and puffy.

The only feature on her face that had escaped the battering were her lips. They were full and kissable. She smiled. Hadn't lost any teeth this round either. She had lost three in previous beatings. She hated losing her teeth. But with her health coverage at W.A.G., she was able to have new caps put on all of them.

She knew that tomorrow she would look a little better

than today. Her eyesight was close to normal again. She had checked herself on the chart in her room. But she was faking it for the doctors so they wouldn't send her home until she was ready.

Yesterday she had walked down to the front door and back so that she would know her way when the time came. Her clothes were in a bag in the bottom of her closet. Last night she had washed the blood off her Green Bay Packers jacket and laid it over the radiator to dry.

She had called Sven last night, and he said he would come and get her whenever she wanted. Just say the word, he told her. He didn't have much to do and so often was looking for ways of keeping busy. She knew it made him feel important that she had called on him for help.

He had hesitantly asked her how she looked.

"Like I got run over by a bulldozer."

"That bad?"

"I think so."

"Who did this to you, Stephanie? You gotta let the police know so they can arrest the guy. I'll testify or whatever I need to do."

Stephanie thanked him, but didn't say much more. She told him she'd call him in the next day or two. After she hung up, she looked out the window and thought about being able to walk down the street and not worry about running into Jack. If he were put away, she could have her life back.

Once again, she was seriously considering telling that woman deputy who had done this to her. Deputy Watkins seemed very reliable, like she might understand what was going on with her. She felt so ashamed of herself for letting a man treat her this way and then going back for more. Rather than talk about it, sometimes it seemed easier to just run away again. But she was starting to realize that it would never end.

She worried that wherever she went, he would find her.

An aide walked in with breakfast. The food at St. Catherine's was as bad as it was in most hospitals, but she was forcing herself to eat it. She needed to get stronger.

Stephanie sat up in a chair, and the aide pushed over the tray on a rolling table.

"Good sign, you sitting up today."

Stephanie didn't say much. She didn't want to get to know these people who were seeing her at her worst. What they must think of her! If she talked to them, they might give her a piece of their mind, and she didn't want anything to do with that.

Stephanie studied the tray—no surprises—Raisin Bran with 2 percent milk, toast, coffee, and juice. It actually looked pretty good.

Just as she was about to take her first bite, someone loomed in her doorway.

"Good to see you up," Deputy Watkins said and walked into the room.

Stephanie pushed her tray away. It would keep. The deputy looked uncomfortable and was still all bundled up with her outdoor clothes on, her jacket zipped way up.

"Is it okay if I close the door?" she asked Stephanie.

Stephanie nodded, surprised at the request.

Watkins closed the door and then unzipped her jacket. A little tawny red head popped out with two bright eyes. The dog let out a yelp that tore her heart open.

Snooper.

The deputy had brought Snooper to visit.

"Oh, baby boy," Stephanie said and reached out her arms for the dog.

Watkins finished unzipping her jacket and then plopped the small dog in his owner's lap.

He stood on her knees and tried to lick her face. She laughed and tried to resist him, not wanting him to jar her nose. After a couple of good licks, he started to settle down.

She petted him and petted him, not believing she was holding him.

"Thank you," she said to Watkins.

"I thought you might want to see him. I know I told you he was okay, but I thought you'd like to see for yourself."

"Yeah, that's true." Stephanie didn't know what to say. She knew she was going to cry, but she didn't want to cry in front of this woman she hardly knew. She felt so vulnerable. Snooper was kind of the only family she had, the only creature that cared about her. He had curled into her lap and made himself right at home. How hard it would be to let him go again.

"Do you want me to step out for a moment?"

"Could you?"

The deputy went out and shut the door behind her.

Stephanie bent her head over and let her blond hair fall on the small dog. Then she cried like she hadn't cried in many years. What would become of her, and how would she protect Snooper from Jack? As the dog licked her hand, she cried harder and felt like something was being torn inside of her. The affection of this small animal ripped her up like the beatings never had.

Stephanie pulled herself together. She stood up, holding the dog tightly, and opened the door. The deputy was standing right outside her door.

Stephanie didn't care if the nurses saw. The rule against dogs in the hospital was stupid. They were cleaner than most people and certainly wouldn't bring in any diseases that were catching to humans.

"Come on back in. I'm okay now. Thank you for bringing Snooper. It just shook me up."

"You've been through a lot. I understand."

Stephanie didn't want to argue about that.

"When are you getting out?" Watkins asked.

"They are going to let me go in another two days, I think.

They just want my eyesight to be back good enough so I can drive. I think they're keeping me in longer since I have no one at home to take care of me."

"Makes sense."

The deputy perched on the edge of the bed, and Stephanie sat back down in the high-backed chair. It was the only chair in the room.

"I went and saw your brother yesterday. He's very concerned about you."

The deputy had talked to her brother. Stephanie was sure he was as charming as he could be. He'd done so well for himself. Big house, new wife. She hated him. Who knows what he had told the deputy? "I bet."

"Do you have anything more to tell me about what happened to you on Thanksgiving?" Watkins asked.

"I really don't. It's all a blur. I've been working on it."

"But Stephanie, you have to know who did this to you."

She wanted to be left alone. "Why do you say that?"

"Because this isn't the first time, is it?"

Stephanie didn't know how to answer her. She didn't want to lie to this woman who had been kind to her.

"I'd like to talk to you about who has done this to you," Claire continued. "I think I can help you. I don't want you to go back home and not be safe."

"I'll be okay. I might go stay with friends or my brother."

The deputy bought it. "Oh, good. I'm glad to hear that."

Stephanie nodded.

"Do you know what you were beaten with?" the deputy asked her.

Stephanie tried to remember what one of the nurses had told her. "A bottle. Some kind of glass bottle."

"Are you sure that's all you know?" The woman deputy was looking at her intently.

Stephanie shook her head.

The deputy stood up and walked over to her. She was

standing too close. It made Stephanie feel very uncomfortable. Then the deputy said, "Your brother knew that it was a champagne bottle. How would he know?"

"Maybe someone else told him. One of the nurses."

The deputy turned away and walked toward the door. Then she asked quietly, "Stephanie, has he ever hurt you?"

"My brother loves me."

"I can't protect you if you won't tell me what's going on. I need you to tell me if your brother had anything to do with this."

"My brother would never hurt me. I'll keep trying to remember."

"Stephanie, I'll give you as much time as you need, but I'm not sure whoever's after you will show you the same courtesy."

Claire sat in her front room, sewing small stitches in cotton fabric. The quilt covered her lap and legs, a hoop pulled tight over a small section of the border. The room was quiet; the night very still. The accumulated snow muffled any noises from the street, but the town, she was sure, had gone to sleep.

Rich had called a while ago, and they had exchanged news of the day. He had a shoulder that was acting up. He had wished she were there to massage it for him. He was working on a small table and chair set for Meg for Christmas. Meg was upstairs sleeping after finishing all her homework. Claire had checked it over.

It was nearly ten-thirty. She wouldn't stay up much longer, but she wanted to get a bit more of the border done.

Somehow she had managed to keep the quilt a secret from Meg. She only worked on it at night when Meg went to sleep. But she was steady at it, working every night for an hour or two.

She would be sorry when the piece was finished. Her fingers were pricked so often they bled, but she found the act of quilting immensely soothing. She could sew and think and not feel wasteful of her time.

Tonight, however, nothing seemed to calm her. She felt twitchy from her inability to find out what had happened to Stephanie Klaus. Someone had to know who was abusing her. She just had to find them. She was getting a weird feeling about John Klaus. Yet he seemed to be the good brother.

Or she had to get Stephanie to talk to her about it. Claire felt like she had made some progress today at the hospital, even if Stephanie had moved away from telling her anything at the end of their conversation. It made her crazy to think about Stephanie: a woman nearly killed who won't tell who was responsible.

Claire came to the end of the thread that was in her needle and made a small knot, then pulled it under the fabric. It held, hidden and secure, tucked into the batting. She threaded her needle again.

What was nice about sewing these small even stitches was that at the end of an hour there were more of them, they added up, and eventually the quilt was done.

In her job, sometimes cases were never finished. Cold cases hung around her neck like so much weight. She did not want Buck's or Stephanie's to be one of them.

Letting her hands fall still, Claire stared out the window. Deep winter. Christmas would be upon them shortly. She saw her own white face reflected in the glass glare over layers of frost.

She remembered a girlfriend of hers from high school looking in the mirror at her house. Tanya. Liquid brown hair down her back. A bruise on her arm. When Claire asked how it had happened, Tanya had rubbed at the mark, then said with a laugh that her boyfriend didn't know his own strength, that he got jealous. She had worn the mark like a badge of their attachment. "He's so good to me afterward. He tells me he loves me all the time."

At that time, Claire hadn't dated anyone seriously and

was surprised at the level of sacrifice a woman might have to endure to be loved. In the way that tragedy can seem romantic when one is young, the bruise seemed like an emblem of love.

She knew better now.

Claire hoped that she could save Stephanie.

19

CLAIRE sat and stared at the top of her desk. Most of it was covered with forms, files, and junk, but there was a clear space between her coffee mug and her Rolodex, and she stared at the bare Formica surface. She was good and stuck.

It was just then that Chief Deputy Sheriff Swanson stopped by. He perched on the edge of her desk, all two hundred and fifty pounds of him. She worried that it might tip, but he seemed to be able to maneuver his bulk around quite well.

"Owens?" he asked. He could be a man of few words. He followed the work of his deputies quite closely, keeping the sheriff filled in on anything important.

"I hate to tell you we're reaching a dead end. Just got the report from WDI that the fingerprint on Buck Owen's glasses matched the bartender's. And we know how that happened. So that lead is gone."

"I can't believe no one in the bar saw anything."

Claire shrugged. "I don't know what to tell you. Trent and

I tracked down everyone, and they don't remember anyone being with him."

"The car?"

"It was pretty well washed out by the lake water."

Stewy didn't say anything for a moment, seeming to chew over what had been said. "So what's next?"

"I still think it's tied into Stephanie Klaus's beating. It's just too much of a coincidence that they were boyfriend and girlfriend, and he gets killed and she nearly does."

"So?"

"She hasn't given me anything. I'm trying to wait her out. I think she is coming to trust me."

"Bring her down to the station?"

"I don't think so. She hasn't done anything wrong."

"Aiding and abetting."

"I don't think that covers conveniently not remembering. She's going to be in the hospital for another day, and I've got one more idea."

What had her uncle, a former cop, told her to do when you hit this dry spot? Look through the cracks, he had always said. Whatever the hell that meant. Probably like reading between the lines in a letter.

"What?"

"The brother's wife. Somehow I just think that Stephanie might be apt to talk to another woman. She doesn't have any friends to speak of. I don't think she and her mom get along that great, but she and her brother have always been close. I thought I would go and try to talk to his new wife. Maybe Stephanie has confided in her."

"Any hunches?"

"Not really. The brother might know something he's not telling. It's hard to say. Stephanie came from one weird family. Then there is Tom Jackson, the cop from Eau Claire. I hate to say it of one of our own, but a lot of cops are abusive."

Swanson grunted and rubbed his chin. "You got work to do. We haven't had many murders in this county, but we've solved every one of them. Thanks to you." He pushed off the desk and walked away.

Claire knew the record. Before she moved down here, there hadn't been a murder in Pepin County for over twenty years.

She was sliding her chair back when Scott walked up to her. He stood in front of her and grinned. She couldn't help but smile back. Nice to have a happy soul around the office.

"Hey," he said.

"Hey to you too," she answered.

"Talked to Billy. He checked out Jackson. Actually called the guy up."

"I'm not sure that's what I wanted him to do."

"Well, whatever. He did it. Jackson claims he hasn't seen Stephanie in many a year. Billy said he didn't sound particularly interested even. Just said the marriage didn't work out."

"Did you find out anything?"

"He's well thought of in the department. Kind of a loner. Does his job. Dependable."

"What about his temper?"

Scott paused, then said, "One guy I talked to said that he'd been known to take off on a perp."

Claire nodded.

"That happens," Scott pointed out.

"Yeah, too often." Claire grabbed her jacket.

"Where you off to?" Scott asked. "A little early for home."

"I wish. I'm going to take care of an evil caretaker."

"Fun."

This was going to be the hard part. The deputy had explained on the phone that possession was indeed nine-tenths of the law. That it would be easier if Mrs. Tabor could try to get the pin back from Lily—steal it back if necessary—before they talked to her. Then they wouldn't have to fight over that.

Lily had the brooch on again today, and it was displayed

on her sweater, which she was still wearing. Mrs. Tabor had snuck down the hallway and turned up the heat a couple degrees. Lily was always fussing about how cold Mrs. Tabor kept the house, but she didn't need to pay the heating bills. However, it would be worth a few extra kilowatts to get her pin back.

Lily was in the kitchen cooking, which was warm work anyway. She was making meatloaf, one of Mrs. Tabor's favorite dishes. Lily didn't make it the way Mrs. Tabor used to, but it was good enough. Mrs. Tabor always liked to put a little horseradish in the ketchup she smeared over the top of the loaf. It gave it a little spark and a bit of color too. But Lily's meatloaf held together better than Mrs. Tabor's ever had. She guessed it was the egg for binding that did it.

"That smells good," Mrs. Tabor commented as Lily put it in the oven.

"Doesn't even smell yet. You must be smelling the oven heating up. Maybe something dripped in there. You better clean the oven one of these days. That's not my job."

"I know. My daughter promised she'd do it next time she came."

Her daughter always promised everything, but she was just too busy to do half the things that needed doing around the house. Sometimes it hurt Mrs. Tabor terribly to see the house fall down around her; other days she didn't mind. They were just getting old together, she figured.

Then Lily did what Mrs. Tabor had been waiting for—she took off her sweater with the pin on it.

Mrs. Tabor didn't look at it. She turned her back in fact and shuffled over to the sink and started fussing around with the dishes. Lily hated when she tried to help. Said she made more of a mess than anything. It was time for Mrs. Tabor to take her nap and Lily to watch her talk shows on TV. Mrs. Tabor had tried to watch them once or twice, but she found it much more stimulating to take a nap.

"You go on now." Lily shooed her away.

Mrs. Tabor walked away from the sink, and Lily took her place. This was her chance. She walked over to the sweater and undid the clasp. It took her a few moments, because her hands were shaking, but the water kept running in the sink. Then the clasp came loose and the pin was in her hand. She set the sweater on the back of the kitchen chair and walked down the hall without looking back.

She knew just where she was going to hide it. Where Lily would never think of looking—in her Bible. Lily was a confirmed atheist. This fact alone should have warned Mrs. Tabor that the woman was not to be trusted. Bad enough not to believe in God, but worse to go around talking about it. She figured that's what confirmed meant. Maybe like confirmation classes she attended in her Lutheran church. Committed to talking about it.

Mrs. Tabor opened her drawer and took out the Bible. The pin made a bump in the pages, but it just looked like she was reading it. Mrs. Tabor put it back in the drawer and lay down on top of the covers on her bed. She knew she wouldn't sleep, but she would rest and pretend. The deputy said she would come right at the end of her shift, close to five o'clock. Lily left by six.

But Mrs. Tabor did sleep, and she dreamed the devil was wearing her pin. Then he grabbed her arm and yelled her name, and she woke up and found Lily next to her bed.

"What did you do with it, you old hag?"

Mrs. Tabor thought she might have preferred her dream to be real. Lily looked like a witch incarnate, her hair hanging over her shoulder, her eyes dark circles of anger.

"Take what?" she asked, trying to pretend she didn't know anything.

Then Lily shook her. "I know what you're up to. You give me things to keep me here, and then you take them away. I won't let you get away with that."

Mrs. Tabor felt sick. The shaking had to stop. She struck out at Lily.

The doorbell rang.

Lily let go of her, and Mrs. Tabor reached out for her glasses, but Lily grabbed them away. "You stay here. I'll take care of whoever it is."

Then Mrs. Tabor prayed. She had been a good Lutheran all her life. She hardly ever asked for anything. She had prayed for Herbert when he was sick, but knew it wouldn't do much good. The cancer had him in its jaws. He was a goner before she had thought to pray. But this time she thought God might hear her.

Lily talked loud, and Mrs. Tabor heard her say that she was lying down, didn't feel good, couldn't see anyone. Then she heard someone walk in and Lily protesting.

"Mrs. Tabor, I'm sorry to hear you're not feeling well." Deputy Watkins was there in the doorway of her room.

"Well, I'd feel a mite better if Lily wouldn't have shaken me so hard." Mrs. Tabor smoothed back her hair. "I need my glasses, Lily."

Lily handed them over. "I didn't know she was coming over again. You didn't say anything. I didn't want her to bother you."

Mrs. Tabor took her time. She had wanted to do this for a long while. She sat up straight on the edge of her bed and put her glasses on. Then she stood up and looked Lily in the face.

"No bother, Lily. I just wanted her here when I told you that you are fired."

Claire was standing right behind Lily and couldn't see her face. First Lily swore. She called Mrs. Tabor a bitch. Then she moved toward Mrs. Tabor. Claire was glad she had positioned herself where she had. Claire stepped in and wrapped an arm around Lily's shoulders from behind, pinning her arms down.

Mrs. Tabor's hands went up to her face. Claire thought how instinctive that move was to protect our eyes, the one part of our body that did not repair itself as well as the rest. Mrs. Tabor cowered.

Lily struggled in Claire's grasp, and then she collapsed against her. "You stupid old woman," she yelled. "Now no one will take care of you."

Mrs. Tabor sat on the edge of her bed and wept.

Claire kept a hand on Lily's shoulder and led her out of the room.

Mr. Turner seemed to be avoiding her this morning. Meg didn't mind too much. It was better than when he was nagging at her, but it did put her teeth on edge. She had done her homework and had done her best on it. But he hadn't looked at their work yet.

The class was quiet, doing a whole page of math problems. Meg did them in her usual fast way, not dawdling the way she had been doing the last few weeks. They got too boring if you did them slow. She had been coming up with an idea in her head, and she wanted to work on it. If she got all her math done, she could stare at the finished problems and think.

Sometimes the numbers even gave her ideas. Last year she had come up with a whole world in her head. Seven was the boy, five was the girl, nine was god, and two and three were the children. Eight was the evil man.

Eight also stood for infinity, a concept that scared her deeply. A number that just went on and on in itself. Sometimes when she was doodling she would draw an eight and then draw an eight in one of the loops and then another eight in one of the smaller loops and see how many eights she could draw. When she realized that if she could draw small enough, she would be drawing eights forever, she felt like she was looking down the mouth of infinity. What went on with no end.

During this difficult time in Mr. Turner's class, she had

realized that she didn't have to always read the stories, that she had a lot of them in her head and that she could follow them there. The stories unrolled in front of her if she let them.

"Meg, could I see you for a few minutes during recess?" Mr. Turner surprised her, coming up behind her.

He would have to tell her that fifteen minutes before they left for recess. Now she would worry for the whole time. She had been working on a story in her head, but it left her when she worried. Then she remembered what she and her mom had talked about, and she was determined to deal with Mr. Turner.

The fifteen minutes went by very slowly. Meg turned in her math paper with everyone else and then watched them all walk out the door. She and Mr. Turner were alone in the room. She walked up to his desk.

"Meg, I had a nice talk with your mother."

Standing this close to him, Meg saw that his eyebrows looked bigger than ever. Meg nodded.

"She and I discussed how you were not working up to your potential."

What a horrible word—potential. Sounded like you were a math equation, and you were supposed to equal something, but you didn't quite make it. She knew people weren't math, even if you could make numbers into characters.

"Meg, do you understand?"

She hadn't realized he wanted her to say anything. "Yes, Mr. Turner."

"Do you agree?"

"I think I've been goofing off a little."

"That has to stop."

She thought his eyebrows looked like two hairy caterpillars, and sometimes she pretended they were about to kiss when he scrunched his forehead, but because the image made her laugh, she tried to avoid it now.

"Your mother and I have agreed that if you do all your

homework and all the class assignments and get your grades up, we will allow you to read in class. But everything has to be done and done well. Do you understand?"

"Yes." Meg was thrilled that she could start reading again. But she wanted to make sure she would not have any more trouble from Mr. Turner for the rest of the year. "I had an idea too."

"What is that, Meg?"

"Well, I was wondering if I could write a story for extra credit."

Mr. Turner smiled. It was not a wonderful sight. He did it so infrequently that it looked like he was in pain. "What a good idea. Do you know what you want to write about?"

What a stupid question. She had a million ideas. Ideas were not the problem, writing them down was. "Yes, I want to write a new fairy tale about a little girl all alone in the woods and how she survives."

20

STEPHANIE was walking through a path in the woods with flowers in bloom all around her. The sky was clear blue like the ocean. She had the feeling that she could fall into it and swim. And Snooper was with her. He was running ahead of her, his tail waving happily like a little flag in a parade.

Then Stephanie woke up into the nightmare that was her life. She lay perfectly still under the crisp sheets of her hospital bed. She was leaving today. The fear that had nestled in her heart like a small animal was uncurling. It was growing into a beast that would be rampaging through her body if she didn't watch it. It would control her and paralyze her. She put her hands over her heart and tried to calm herself. Think of water, she told herself, the calm, lazy water of summer. She tried and tried, but it turned to ice in the eyes of her mind.

She took deep breaths and forced herself into the world that surrounded her. She had to get up and get going. She could feel the fear pound gently in her blood, getting her to move.

Stephanie checked the clock on the wall. She could see it pretty well. Her eyes were a lot better. Eight-thirty. Breakfast was sitting next to the bed. She must have slept through them bringing it in.

She had asked Sven to come around ten o'clock. That would give her time to take a bath and get everything ready. She had told the nurse that she wanted to put on regular clothes today. She had cleaned her clothes and had them sitting in the bottom of the closet. It was no secret she was leaving the hospital. She just didn't want everyone to know. Like her brother.

That was a laugh—what a brother he had turned out to be.

He had even asked her to come and stay with him. She wouldn't stay with him in a million years, especially not since he had married that woman he called his wife. She was a moron and deserved exactly what she had walked into. But she didn't know a thing.

Stephanie gently lifted her feet over the side of the bed. She heard a man moaning down the hall. He had been singing hymns last night. She almost liked the moaning better; it was more rhythmical. Standing up felt okay. Her head didn't keep going after her body stopped. Today it felt attached to her neck.

She walked cautiously to the bathroom, but everything stayed level around her. She had slept well last night, and her dream had been a wonderful present this morning.

When she looked in the mirror, she saw that the bruising was running down her face like old mascara. A dark blue smudge sat high on her cheekbones like the smear football players wear to keep the sun from reflecting into their eyes. Jack had explained its use to her one day when they were watching TV.

She needed to stop thinking about him. He had to come to matter less than nothing to her. In a few days, he would be miles away from her, getting farther away all the time. Maybe she'd move to China. Whatever was the total opposite place on Earth—as far away as one could possibly get—that's where she'd go.

She washed her face and got out a bottle of Cover Girl makeup that one of the nurses had picked up for her from the drugstore down the street. Stephanie called it Cover-Up makeup. She put a blob under each eye and let it soak in, then rubbed it carefully to smooth it out. Her face looked much less scary. She could almost pass on the street for a normal woman, not one that was battered all the time.

Then a nurse came walking in, bringing a bouquet of flowers. "Lookit what you got."

Stephanie looked at the flowers—pink and red carnations—and felt like throwing up. She saw the card sitting nestled in among the blossoms and didn't dare open it. But maybe they weren't from him.

The red-haired nurse set the flowers down on the rolling table and smiled as if she were responsible for them being there.

Stephanie made herself walk over and smell the flowers. Carnations had such a good smell—clean and sweet at the same time. She picked up the card and opened it.

"Sorry to hear about your troubles. Hope you get better. Your ex, Tommy."

Shit.

In front of the nurse's astonished eyes, she dropped the bouquet in the wastebasket with a good thud. The nurse left without saying anything.

Stephanie sat down and ate her breakfast. She forced herself to eat every last bite. Even the oatmeal, which reminded her of gruel she had read about as a kid in books where children were left alone in the woods and found by witches.

Then she dressed. Another nurse bustled in and took her vitals, telling her everything looked fine.

"Are you leaving us?" the nurse asked.

"I think so."

"Your face looks so much better today."

"I helped it along."

"Don't we all, sweetie."

Stephanie liked it that the woman had called her sweetie. Her mother had never been one for endearments, and Jack had called her "bitch" and "babe" more than he'd said her name. If she ever had kids, she would kiss them every day and tell them how much she loved them. Buck had called her "Stuff." It was cute the way he said it. Sometimes he called her "Hot Stuff." She wished he were still around. If she had told him about Jack, maybe he would have been more prepared and could have protected himself. Maybe he would have protected her.

She felt herself starting to cry. She had to stop that. But any way she looked at it, Buck's death was her fault. She had almost called him "honey" once. But she had been scared to get close to him. There were lots of things she wished she would have said to him, but it was all gone now.

Snooper wasn't gone. She could hardly wait to see him again. He was her little Poopla, her Gentleman.

When Sven walked in her room, she was all ready to go, sitting on the edge of her bed.

She could tell he was afraid to look at her. But when he finally did, he smiled and said, "Hey, you look pretty good."

"Not too bad."

They made her ride in a wheelchair, and a big black guy pushed her out the door with Sven carrying a bag that held her washbasin and other accoutrements. As the nurse said to her, she had paid for them, she might as well take them.

Sven made sure she was warm and comfortable in the car. He waited while she put her seat belt on. He drove slow and careful as they left Durand and headed down toward the lake on Highway 35. It was about half an hour to home. She couldn't wait to see Snooper. They were going to stop on their way and pick him up. She had called Rich Haggard, and he said he'd be there all morning. He said Snooper had been a good dog, but was waiting for her. When she asked how he knew the dog was waiting for her, he said, "Because he often sits facing the door, waiting for someone to come in. I think it's you."

Sven cleared his throat.

She turned and looked at him, knowing he wanted to say something.

"How're you feeling?" he asked.

"Better."

"I'm sorry about what happened to you."

"Thanks."

"Claire, the deputy, came and asked me if I knew anything about what went on that day, but I didn't. I just found you, and I thought you might be dead. I hate to say it, but you looked so bad."

"Sven, you've been a good friend to me. Thanks for taking care of everything."

"I didn't do much. The dog wouldn't let me near. I just called Claire. I have to tell you, I was scared for you."

"Yeah, I'm sorry you had to see that."

"Don't mind that." He puffed out his breath. "But she made it sound like you hadn't told her who did it. Don't you know who did it? We have to find that guy. I'd wring his neck myself."

"He's not worth it, Sven. The best thing to do with him is ignore him." She had to tell him something.

"I don't believe that, Stephanie. He needs to be put away. He's a menace out in society. Have you told Claire who it is?"

"Not yet."

"But you will?"

"If I have to."

"I hope you do."

Snooper was standing on his back legs on a footstool that Rich had placed by the window for him. Somehow the dog knew that Stephanie was coming and he was hard at work, waiting for her.

Rich didn't question this knowledge. He had worked with animals for too long to doubt their abilities to discern things that humans could not notice.

He realized he would miss the little dog when he left, even though Snooper had made it clear that he was only a guest and that his true home was with another. Maybe he should get a dog. He had been thinking about it for a few years and had been almost to the point of buying one when he met Claire.

It sounded stupid but he could admit to himself that he hadn't bought a dog because of her. He wanted to know what their living arrangement would be before he brought a dog into his life. If they were going to live together in the near future, he would rather wait and buy a dog with Claire and Meg, a dog that would be all of theirs, a dog that would begin to make them a family.

But he hadn't brought up marriage yet with Claire. He was giving her time to recover from the death of her husband and the other tragedies in her life. And there was his own slight indecision. Sometimes she seemed like a lot to take on. But usually he saw that he did not want to live without her.

Sven's old Valiant pulled up in front of the house. Snooper's tail was going as fast as an eggbeater. The little dog jumped down off the stool when he saw Stephanie step out of the car. Rich opened the door for Snooper, and he bounded down the steps and scampered across the driveway, flinging himself at Stephanie's legs. But only for a moment. Then the blond woman bent down and scooped him up.

Rich turned away for a moment and put some water on the stove to heat up. He had felt tears rise to his eyes and didn't like the feeling of crying so easily. He set out a couple coffee mugs.

Sven came tromping up the stairs.

"Cup of coffee?" Rich asked.

"Don't mind if I do."

Rich figured as much. Sven was sometimes a little hard pressed to find things to keep himself busy. He and Rich had joined an informal group of men who gathered once a week to work on wood. Some carved bird whistles, some carved spoons, some made small boxes. They talked about the weather and a little about politics, but gently. They didn't want any rancor in their midst. Sven had been making wooden flowers but was starting to branch out into bird-houses, painting them some wild colors. He was talking about selling them at the garden store in the spring.

Stephanie came up the steps but stopped at the door.

"Come on in," Rich told her.

"I should get home."

"Stop for a moment. I've got coffee on."

She looked ready to resist, and then Snooper licked her right on the lips, and she laughed. "Okay. I can't thank you enough for taking care of Snooper."

"Yes, you can. One thanks is enough. That's one smart dog you got there. He was a perfect guest."

"He was my boyfriend's."

"So I heard." Rich had decided that he wasn't going to press Stephanie for any information. He knew, from talking to Claire, that she was being closemouthed about who had beaten her up. But he figured she'd tell when she was ready. She just needed people close around her who she could trust. By taking care of her dog, he figured he had shown her where he stood. She could tell him whatever she wanted to. He was there.

"It's strong coffee," he told her. "So there's cream and sugar if you need to tone it down."

"It's so strong, it'll put hair on your chest," Sven told her.

She sat down at the table and held the mug in her hand as if she were gathering warmth from it. Snooper curled up in her lap.

"Another storm's coming in," Sven said.

Stephanie's head jerked up. "When?" she asked.

"They say soon. What'd they know? They thought the last one would be worse than it was. But we're having a real, true winter this year. Just like we used to have when I was a kid."

Stephanie doctored up her coffee with both cream and sugar. Rich took the opportunity to look her over. She was a pretty woman, but she did look a little damaged at the moment. It wasn't just the bruises under her eyes. It was the way she held herself, pulled in, shoulders hunched, arms over chest, head tucked down. She took a sip of her coffee as if someone might grab it away from her. He thought of reaching out and patting her arm, but didn't think she was ready for any man to touch her. He thought of asking her to stay with him—even though he knew that would be totally inappropriate, as they said these days. But he hated the thought of her going back to her house on her own.

"I thought you were going to go stay with your brother," he said.

Her head lifted like a deer hearing a noise in a meadow. "Never."

When Claire walked out into the cold, she felt her shoulders automatically rise against it. Living with this intense cold must be like living with constant battering. You cringe. It made you fear the assault of the outdoors. But there was always the promise that it would eventually be over. Right now, she didn't dare think of spring. It would make her yearn for warmth that was still too far off.

When she got into her car, she questioned what she was doing—driving all the way back down to Winona—but she had called Mrs. Klaus and told her she would be there in the early afternoon. The weather was threatening them with another big storm: over a foot of snow and gusts of wind up to fifty miles an hour. Those gusts meant that drifts would form across roads that vehicles couldn't drive through. But the weather wasn't predicted to come in until after nightfall. That was five hours away. Time enough for her to scoot down to Winona and back.

The river was still open below Lake Pepin, and the water steamed as it meandered through the locks of the small river towns: Alma, Fountain City, then Winona. It took her only an hour because the roads were good.

The Klaus house was an old Victorian, but fully restored in excellent shape with a new paint job—dark green siding with a deep maroon trim. Handsome. Fifteen years ago, they were giving these houses away. Now this one would bring in a bundle.

When Claire rang the doorbell, no one answered right away. She knocked once more, and then, as she was about to turn away, the door creaked open.

A tall, thin brown-haired woman answered it. She was probably around twenty-five, wearing a turtleneck and jeans with the grace of a model. She was dressed neatly, but there was something unkempt about her. Then Claire saw that it was her hands. The nails were bitten down to the quick, and the knuckles looked raw and worried.

Claire showed the young woman her ID and asked, "Mrs. Klaus? I called you earlier."

"Yes, I know. I told John you were coming. He said to let him know when you arrived. Please call me Eugenia."

"May I come in?" Claire suggested, as Mrs. Klaus made no move to usher her in.

"Excuse me while I call my husband." The woman left Claire standing in the entryway. A large stairway curled around to the second floor. It was all open, and the bannister was a lovely dark wood, polished to a glow.

In the living room, a dark oriental rug lay in front of the fireplace; a bay window overlooked the street. The house was immaculate and could have served as a movie setting for a turn-of-the-century drama.

Eugenia walked back in. "He said to show you in. He'll be

here in a few minutes. It's time for him to come home for lunch, so this works out well."

"That really wasn't necessary. I've actually come to talk to you."

"Oh." Eugenia led the way into the living room. It looked more like what used to be called a parlor. Thick red curtains hung in the windows, giving a sense of richness and elegance to the dark room. Eugenia offered her a chair. It was a big brown leather chair that smelled of cigar smoke when Claire sank into it. Opposite her, Eugenia stretched out on a dark green velvet couch.

"You have a lovely home."

"We're very proud of it. John bought it before we were married. He's done most of the work on it. I believe Stephanie lived here for a while." She twisted the ring on her hand. "You know, John and I have only been married a year, so the house is really his doing."

Claire hadn't realized that the siblings were that close. "Did she live here after her divorce?"

"I believe so. John doesn't talk about it much. He was building up his practice. He's a lawyer. He did some work for my father. That's how we met."

"What do you do?"

Eugenia brought her hands back up to her chest, folding them as if in prayer. "I keep the house. I'm an old-fashioned wife. That's the way John likes it. There is so much work to do around here. He is very particular."

"You're doing a great job. I can imagine what a lot of work a house like this might be."

Eugenia brought her hands down to her lap. "Thank you. I do my best."

"I'd like to ask you about Stephanie."

Eugenia started and looked as if she had heard something other than the question Claire had just asked her. "What?" she asked.

"Stephanie. How well do you know her?"

"Hardly at all. If you want to know the truth, I don't think she likes me. We haven't seen her at all for quite a few months. John says she's jealous. I don't know what it is. I've tried to be nice to her. She is so pretty."

"Has he told you what has happened to Stephanie?"

"Only that she got hurt. He said that this wasn't the first time something like this had happened to her."

"He said that? Did he mention who had done it to her before?"

Suddenly the door opened, and John Klaus walked in, dressed in the full uniform of the professional working man—three-piece suit and a dark wool gabardine coat. Eugenia stood up and went to him, taking his coat to hang up in the closet. As they stood next to each other for a moment, Claire was struck by what a handsome couple they made. Then John walked into the living room and stood over her.

He asked immediately, sounding a little worried, "Deputy, what brings you here again? Nothing has happened to Stephanie, has it? I tried to call her a few minutes ago, and they tell me she's left the hospital."

"Really? I think she's fine. She was when I saw her last night. I thought she wasn't leaving until tomorrow."

His face darkened. "That is quite like Stephanie. She changes her mind. But I don't like the thought of her being on her own. I had hoped she'd stay with us."

"No. I agree that she shouldn't be on her own. I suggested the shelter in Durand, but she resisted it, I think because of the dog. But I live in Fort St. Antoine close by her. I will drive by and see her when I get off work. Maybe I can persuade her to come and stay with you for a while at least."

"Officer, you've done enough. I can take care of this. I'll check in on her this afternoon. Don't worry." He looked back at his wife. She was standing in the doorway, hovering.

Claire remained seated even though her two hosts were standing. "I've actually come to talk to your wife. I had thought I'd made that clear. I'm sorry if there's been a confusion."

"Talk to her about what?"

"Well, Stephanie. Sometimes women confide in other women. I'm getting nothing out of Stephanie, and I felt it was worth a try. They are sisters-in-law."

He turned quickly toward his wife, and her hands flew to her face. "My wife barely knows my sister. To tell you the truth, I don't think Stephanie cares for her. I'd be very surprised if she would tell her anything. Isn't that right, Genie?"

Eugenia nodded and lowered her hands. Watching her husband's face, she said, "I don't think I can tell you anything about her. I really don't know her at all."

John Klaus inclined his head like the gracious host, fitting into the setting as if he had been born to it. "I'm sorry you had to come all this way for nothing."

21

S VEN walked around the side of the car and opened the door for Stephanie. She set Snooper down on the ground, and he scampered up the path to the house. As she stood up, Sven took her arm so she wouldn't slip on the packed snow.

She pulled away. "I'm okay."

"Let me help you," Sven said as they walked up to the door of her house. He stayed a careful yard away from her.

"You've done enough." Stephanie looked around. Snooper was at the door already, lifting one paw up, then the other, prancing in the cold. "You cleared off my whole driveway."

"I used the snowblower."

Stephanie smiled at him. She had such a sweet smile. It reminded him of no one else. She always looked like she was smiling only for him.

"You dug out my car."

"It wasn't in very deep," he protested, even though the car had taken him three hours of slow, careful work, checking his pulse as he went.

"You came to get me at the hospital. Thank you so much. I hope someday I'll be able to repay you."

"Just get better. I need to see your smiling face around town."

He had hoped she would invite him in, but he could tell she wasn't going to. She had stopped to tell him all this a few feet in front of her door. She stood on her tiptoes, leaned in, and kissed him on the cheek.

"Thanks, Sven. Bye-bye." She turned, walked to her door, and let Snooper run in the house before she followed.

He hated to let her stay in the house by herself. Watching the door shut, he gave up for a moment. He headed back to his car, thinking there was nothing he could do. She wanted to be on her own, that's the way it would be.

He stood and turned his face up. The sky was as soft a white as the underside of an old wool blanket. It looked like it was going to start snowing hard pretty soon. He could feel it in the air and in his bones. Then he'd have an excuse to call her and come over. She'd need her driveway cleared out again. Maybe he'd bring her something. Some flowers, or something to eat. She looked thin to him.

He climbed into his car and had a laugh at himself. She was a young woman. Why would she want to have anything to do with an old codger like him? He was close to sixty, with a bad heart. A lonely man who had to work hard to keep busy. He hadn't a thing to offer her but his kindness.

But he figured she needed that as bad as she needed anything. She didn't look like she had gotten her share of kindness in her life.

He drove out onto the highway, thinking he'd bring in some wood for a fire. Heat up some soup and settle in by the window for a good storm. He would read, but mainly he would stare out the window. He had become more reflective as he aged. When he was working full time for 3M, he never had time to do much serious thinking, just worried about the business. Now he thought a lot about philosophical questions, like what life was all about. He wondered what Stephanie thought about life.

Driving back to Durand, Claire felt itchy. It was a feeling she got when something wasn't sitting right with her. John Klaus had given her such a feeling. And his wife, his self-effacing wife.

Eugenia seemed to be holding tenuously onto her life, her small hands working constantly to protect her face. Timid and threatened, she tiptoed around when her husband was there in their perfect house. What was the story with the two of them?

Maybe that strained relationship was why Stephanie hadn't wanted to stay with them. Maybe her brother did take after their father and was abusing his wife. Maybe Claire was reading too much into everything.

But as she remembered the way Eugenia had moved through the house, had held her hands in front of her body, had reacted to any movement from her husband, Claire was reminded of Mrs. Tabor. Cowering. She became certain that Eugenia was being abused by her husband.

At first, she had thought she was leaving Winona with nothing, but now another fact that she learned was pricking her. Stephanie and John had lived together recently, after Stephanie's divorce. Claire decided she needed to do more checking on John Klaus. Maybe he resembled his father in more ways than looks.

The snow started to fall just as she pulled into the lot by the sheriff's department. Big thick flakes fluttered down, covering the dark spots on the street. The world would go white again. She didn't want to stay in the office long. It was time to head home. But she wanted to check on John Klaus before she left. In her background checks on Stephanie, she hadn't looked at her brother.

Scott was walking out as she came in. "Stewy says we're

all to go home if we're not on duty tonight. Storm coming in doesn't look good."

"Shoot. I heard we might be getting something." Claire said good night to him and walked to the communication center and got on a computer.

She pulled up what she could on the databases. Everything seemed to be working slow. She hated it when the machine ground on, not spitting out the information that she wanted. Finally she found the right John Klaus. John Klaus, no criminal record, speeding ticket four years ago. Father, James Klaus, mother Ginnie Klaus. That name sounded wrong. That wasn't the name of Stephanie's mother.

She pulled out her file on Stephanie. When she compared the two sets of information, she realized John and Stephanie weren't really siblings. Stephanie's father was not James Klaus. Her mother had married him when Stephanie was six and John was ten. James Klaus had adopted Stephanie, and she had taken his name.

Stephanie and John were not birth brother and sister. They had lived together a few years ago. Their father abused his wife and Stephanie. What had John learned from all this?

There was one other thing that had been bothering Claire. John Klaus had walked in to his house impeccably dressed, but one item had been missing from his ensemble. He hadn't worn a scarf with his coat, which was open at the collar.

On a hunch Claire made a phone call.

Eugenia answered the phone in her quiet voice, "Klaus residence," sounding more like a maid than the lady of the house.

"Mrs. Klaus, I'm sorry to bother you again, but when I was leaving your house, I found a brown cashmere scarf on the ground by my car. It was buried in the snow. Did you lose one?"

"Oh, thank goodness." Genuine relief sounded in Eugenia's voice. "That's my husband's. He's been so upset about losing it. I'll tell him you found it as soon as he gets back."

John Klaus had told Claire that he hadn't been to see Stephanie in months. But the scarf had been only lightly covered with snow. He had known that Stephanie was hit with a champagne bottle, which was not common knowledge.

"Where did he go?" Claire asked, afraid she knew the answer.

"To get Stephanie."

Rich walked down to the road to watch the snow fall out of the sky. He couldn't see across the lake; he couldn't even see the lake. The snow quieted the world. There were a few cars driving slowly by on the highway—people trying to get home before the snowstorm shut everything down. The plows wouldn't be out for hours. They would probably wait until morning to attack the streets. No sense getting caught out in the middle of the storm.

Last he heard, they were saying they might get over a foot of snow. On top of what they already had on the ground, it would make an impressive pile.

Maybe he should go and pick up Meg. He knew she was at the house of Ramah, her baby-sitter. It would be one less thing Claire would have to do when she got home. He felt lonely in his house—no dog, no women. He'd rather be snowed in at Claire's than alone at his own home.

He'd filled a Crock-Pot full of the makings for chili in the morning, and it was starting to smell pretty good. He could just bring that in the car, and dinner would be ready. He and Meg could make some cornbread, heat up the house. A perfect night at home by the fire. It was becoming more common for him to spend most nights with Claire and Meg.

As he was walking into his house, he heard the phone ring, but he didn't get to it in time to answer it. He should get an answering machine or something, but he couldn't be bothered.

But the unanswered call made him think of his neighbor—Stephanie. He wondered how she was doing back in her house. He picked up his phone, looked up her number, and dialed it.

After a few rings, her tentative voice answered. "Hello?"

"Hi, Stephanie. It's Rich. I just wanted to be sure you were doing all right. Have you got enough food and everything?"

"I'm fine."

"'Cause it's starting to come down pretty hard."

"The house has warmed up nicely."

"How's Snooper?"

"He's curled up in a ball on his favorite blanket."

"Good."

"Thanks for your concern. Don't worry about me."

22

STEPHANIE usually loved a winter storm. Always a good excuse to curl up inside and work on her weaving. But she wished this one would hold off for a while. She looked out the window and saw the flakes coming down. She wanted the car warmed up before they left, so she threw on her down parka and ran out to turn on the car.

The cold took her breath away. She couldn't really run in it. She hunkered down inside her jacket, pulling the hood over her head and breathing through the fur ruff like a wolf.

When she got to the car, she had trouble opening the driver's-side door. It was frozen shut. After trying all the doors, she finally was able to pull the back left door open and crawl over into the front seat. She put the key in the ignition, said a short prayer, and cranked it. Nothing. Stone dead. Not a whisper of a growl. When it was this cold, she usually plugged her car in. It had sat for days with no one starting it, and it sounded like the battery was drained.

She slammed her hand against the steering wheel and said, "Shit." Then she stared out at the windshield. The snow was already covering everything so completely, she could hardly see out of the car.

No one could get to her in all this weather. She would be safe in her house for a while. She would wait out the storm, get her car's battery charged up, and be off before Jack came to find her.

She slammed her shoulder against the car door, and it popped open with the sound of a tree branch breaking under a weight of ice. The wind took the door and blew it back, almost to the point of snapping it off the car. No one would be on the road in this weather. She grabbed her small carry-on case and brought it back into the house with her. It had all her neccessities. She was sure there was a can of Campbell's bean with bacon soup in the cupboard she could heat up. Snooper was fine for dog food. They would have a good rest tonight and start out tomorrow morning, bright and early.

As she trudged back up to the house, she wished she would have done something more for Sven Slocum. He was such a nice older man. Kept himself in pretty good shape and always had a kind word to say to everyone. She might need to call him about the battery. She could try to bring it into the house and warm it up. She had heard that worked sometimes.

She hustled back into the house and found Snooper sitting watching the door. She rubbed the little dog's head. "Don't worry. You won't be rid of me so easy this time. We're sticking together like glue."

Stephanie put on her moonboots and found her heavy leather choppers. After scrounging through her junk drawer, she found a small screwdriver and stuck that in her pocket. She wrapped a big long red scarf around her hood and over her face. Snooper started barking at her.

"I have to go outside one more time. Then we'll snuggle in here. Don't you worry."

She braved the wind and cold again. After releasing the hood latch inside the car, she lumbered up to the front of the car and pulled open the hood. She looked down at the battery.

What did she know? It looked fine. She was scared to do this, but thought it was her only chance to not involve someone else. She always hated to ask for help.

She had watched Jack work on his car. He had shown her how to do things, like change the oil. He had replaced batteries for her. He had done so many good things for her. What was really weird was that once in a while she still had the impulse to call him for help. He had always been there for her. Her whole life.

He had stepped in between her and her stepfather and saved her from a beating. With that action, Stephanie had fallen in love with him, although she had loved him for a long time. He was her big brother and so handsome. Coming home in his uniform, he looked like Richard Gere in *An Officer and a Gentleman.*

After they had started to sleep together, he wanted to take her out to a dance one night. When she saw that he had put on his uniform, she laughed. No one wore a uniform out in public anymore. That was the first time he had slugged her. Crack, right across the mouth, right while she was still laughing. One sharp smack. It left bruises on her cheeks, but startled her more than hurt her. "Don't ever laugh at me," he had said.

She pulled her mind away from Jack and back to the problem of the battery. The removal looked pretty straightforward. She unclipped the two battery cables from the posts and loosened the clamp with her bare hand, finding the choppers too clumsy to manuever. Then she carefully lifted out the battery.

A roar came up behind her and she almost dropped the battery.

She thought someone had driven into her driveway and quickly turned to be ready to confront them, but it was only the wind and a gust of snow. The storm was strengthening. She took a deep breath and carried the battery up to the house.

Snooper growled and barked at the battery, but she just laughed at him and set it down on the plastic mat that she had next to the door for her boots. Then she found a big cardboard box and covered it so that Snooper couldn't get at it.

"Stay away from that. Not good for you."

Snooper danced around her until she swooped him up in her arms. "How about some soup?" she asked and he licked her face.

Rich didn't answer the phone. Maybe he had gone to get Meg. He often did that for her. Meg loved hanging out with him. Claire wished she were there right now. She longed to go home and sink into the family setting with Meg and Rich, but she had a very bad feeling about Stephanie. Claire was afraid her so-called brother John was after her.

Claire tried to call Stephanie, but she didn't answer the phone either. No answering machine. Where could she be in this weather? Maybe she had gone over to Sven's to stay. That would solve everything.

Then a horrible thought struck her. What if John Klaus was there already? What if she had been badly hurt by him?

The office had just about cleared out. Judy, who lived close by, was manning the phones. "Judy, could you try to get Scott and ask him to meet me at Stephanie Klaus's house, in Fort St. Antoine?"

"Does he know where it is?"

"Yes. Keep trying until you get him. I'll check back in with you on my way home."

"Good luck getting there."

Claire stepped out of the courthouse, and the wind slammed into her.

"Man alive," she whispered under her breath. Visibility was already bad. She could hardly see across the street. She got into her patrol car and was glad she had used it so recently and it was all warmed up. The windows dripped from the snow falling on them. She cleared the windshield and started down the road.

Driving in this heavy snow was bad enough, but what made it worse was that a small slick of ice was forming beneath the snow on the road, which made it really slippery. She had to drive slowly to avoid spinning off the road. Her headlights punched two small holes in the swirling whiteness. Car headlights came upon her moments before they passed her. There was no room for mistakes in this white world.

It took her twenty-five minutes to reach Highway 35. Usually she made it in fifteen. The snow was coming down heavier, and it was piling up on the roads. The wind was starting to drift the snow across the roads. At least she was driving down in the valley and not up on top of the bluffs, where the drifts could shut the roads down in no time at all.

She stopped to call in to Judy to ask if she had been able to get through to Scott. She was going to ask her to call Stephanie also, but when she got through, Judy told her the phone lines were down around Durand.

"This is going to be a bad one," Judy said and added, "Let me know when you get home."

Claire told her to keep trying Scott on his car phone and signed off. She started to inch her way northward. She was very conscious of being in a little metal box on wheels while the wind buffeted her around. All that was protecting her from the elements was this vehicle.

Finally she drove into Pepin. The faint lights of the town were welcoming, but she had to keep going. She swung by Scott's house, but there was no patrol car out front. She wondered if he had stopped for a drink on the way home. She didn't have time to find out where he was. She had to get to Stephanie's.

Back into the dark whiteness. Night had fallen. If she turned her brights on, it made the visibility worse. The snow became a huge swarm of white insects peppering the darkness. She kept her low beams on and tried to follow the road. It was exhausting to watch for the faint trail of tire tracks in the white snow.

Jack rode the storm up the river. His anger fizzed in his arms and legs and sparked in his head. Stephanie was trying to get away again. He knew it. What was the matter with her? She knew as well as he did that they belonged together.

She had given herself to him when she was only fifteen and a virgin. He and Stephanie had grown up together since she was six and he was ten. They were told they were brother and sister, but he always knew better. He always knew there was something between them that was explosive.

She had been such a pretty little girl, blond hair a halo around her head. His real mom, the one who had run away and left him with his father, had called him Jack, and he had liked it. Everyone else called him John. But Stephanie knew how much he liked to be called Jack, and she had always called him that. Even when she was mad at him.

When he was seventeen, he had dropped out of high school and enlisted in the marines. All his life, his father had told him that he was a worthless piece of shit. So Jack knew that his father wouldn't help him go to school. His father took every opportunity he could to tell Jack just how stupid he was. He was sent to basic training and had not returned to his home for a couple of years. He knew the marines was the only way he was going to get ahead, that he would never have the resources to go to college without the extra training he would get in the service.

A couple of years later, he had come back to stay with his family while he was on leave, and there was Stephanie, all grown up and beautiful as a beauty queen. No one had ever even kissed her. Then he found out his dad was slapping Stephanie around.

One night Jack had stepped in and told the old man to lay

off Stephanie if he knew what was good for him. His dad had come at him, and the many hours of working out stood Jack in good stead. He dropped his father with a right punch and then kicked the shit out of him. Stephanie cried and threw herself in Jack's arms. He had wanted to take her right there.

A few days later he had gone into her room when their parents were out of the house. She had welcomed him into her bed. He showed her all the ways of sex that he had learned from the whores he had gone to with his buddies. He had never been with a real clean woman before. He had almost felt like it was his first time too.

He had promised her they would be together all their lives. Then he had to report back, and while he was gone, she married some jerk. But as soon as he was back in her life, she dumped that guy for him. That's how much they had meant to each other. They had lived together in Winona for a while. Then she had run away. He didn't want to think about that.

His own marriage was a sham—just something he had done when Stephanie had left him last year. It didn't mean anything. Eugenia was worthless. She cringed around him like a dog, and like a dog, she deserved to be kicked. At least Stephanie stuck up for herself.

He liked driving in this kind of wild and rough weather. He had bought his Lincoln Navigator so that nothing could stop him when he wanted to move. The car had been ridiculously expensive, but that was one of the things that Jack liked about it. He could afford it. His business was going very well.

He would be with Stephanie soon. He had driven through Pepin a while ago. Even though it was slow going, he should be at her house any moment.

He saw the first big house on the edge of Fort St. Antoine. Stephanie's house was the one after that. He slowed as he came to her driveway. Someone had plowed her out. Her car was parked in the middle of the driveway. He pulled in behind it so she couldn't get away.

This time they could really start all over. This time he

would take care of her and persuade her that they should be together. She would come home with him, he would kick Eugenia out on her butt. It would be the way it was supposed to be. She would love him again like she had when she was fifteen. That's all he had ever wanted.

He would get Stephanie back one way or another. He would do whatever he had to do. She would be his forever.

Meg loved the snow. This snow was perfect and fluffy. Not good for snowballs, but excellent for snow angels. On the walk home from Ramah's, she had taken mounds of it and thrown it up into the air. By the time she reached her house with Rich, she was covered with it.

"Stand still and let me brush you off." Rich stepped in, grabbed an old broom off the porch, and proceeded to sweep her down. Meg got the giggles and almost collapsed back into the snow.

"What a goof you are," he said, holding her up by the hood of her jacket.

"Can we play poker tonight?" she asked.

Rich had been teaching her how to play poker. They could usually persuade her mom to join them. They used pennies from a big jar to bet, playing different games with names like "Spit in the Ocean" and "Criss-Cross." Mom still needed to look at the list of the order of the hands, but Meg pretty much knew when she had a good hand. They didn't happen that often.

"We'll see."

"Now you sound like my mom."

"Your mother is a wise woman."

As soon as they stepped into the house, the phone rang. Meg slid out of her boots and ran to answer it.

"I've got it," she shouted to Rich.

"Hello, Watkins residence," she said. "This is Meg speaking."

"Is your mom there?" a woman's voice asked.

"No, not yet. We expect her shortly. Can I ask who's calling?"

"Just tell her Stephanie said it's her brother." Meg didn't understand the message, but she could tell that the woman was upset.

"Your brother?"

"Yes, just tell her. He's come to get me." She hung up.

23

AFTER she hung up the phone, Stephanie saw that Jack was nearly at the front door. She had locked it as soon as she saw the car turn in the driveway. Thank God she had been in the kitchen when he had come, or he could have walked right in on her.

Snooper had heard the car and was going crazy barking. She had to take care of him immediately, her first concern.

She swooped the dog up in her arms and ran to the bedroom, where she had left the crate for him in the closet. She pushed him into the crate, shut the crate, closed the closet, closed the door to the room, and ran back to the kitchen.

Jack was pounding on the front door. Then he started crashing into it. She didn't know how long it would last. This house wasn't built for battering. She put her down jacket back on and slipped into her moon boots. When she looked again at what he was doing, she saw he had picked up a flower pot she had left sitting on the steps from last summer and was slamming it into the window in the door. On his third try, the small window shattered, and glass flew everywhere.

Stephanie backed out of the room. His hand came in the window and he tried to reach down to the door knob. She thought of fighting him off, but the stronger instinct in her was to flee. She went out the back door and circled around the house. She wanted to get him away from the house so Snooper would be safe.

Stephanie ran down the driveway. When she was at the road, she turned back. Jack had seen her and had jumped off the steps of the house and was coming after her.

She ran. She had always been a good runner, but the combination of moon boots and a half foot of powder snow didn't increase her speed. But it wouldn't help Jack either. She knew her way in this white, snowy world better than he did, and she knew where she was headed. She hoped the snow would shroud the way and that he would give up and leave them alone.

But if not, she was headed toward safety—Sven's house on the edge of the park. She knew he was there and would let her in. Jack would not want a witness to his anger and would leave her be—if she could reach Sven's house without Jack catching up to her.

It was hard to run in the storm. She tucked her head down into her chest, only lifting it occasionally to see her way. The streetlights were blurry white balls of light. She could hear Jack behind her, and she picked up her speed, not allowing herself to look back at him. She was running as fast as she could. It would do her no good to see him gaining on her.

She cut across the street and knew she was only a block away from Sven's house. She couldn't see it yet. Then she saw his outdoor light. She ran toward it. As she came up to his house, she saw that he had already shoveled his walk once. The snow was filling it in. When she got to the door, she banged on it. Looking back, she could see that Jack was only a half a block away. She could see his vague moving form.

"Stephanie," he called.

She turned and banged again. She tried the door. It was locked. Damn, why would Sven lock his door? Jack would be upon her in a few moments. She couldn't stay pounding on the door.

She jumped off the steps and made her mistake. Instead of turning toward town, she turned toward the lake and ran.

Sven had just finished taking a long, hot shower and was doing his rendition of "Camelot"—his wife and he had seen the play in New York with the original cast, and he imagined himself as Robert Goulet—and tying his shoes when he heard the pounding on his front door.

Who the hell could that be? Probably Arne from down the street wanting to play hearts. Sven hated hearts. He never won, and he could be a bad loser. But he did have a six-pack of beer in the fridge, and he hated to drink alone. He had done that a few times after his wife died, but never found it satisfying. But he wasn't sure that's the way he wanted to spend the evening—drinking with Arne.

Arne didn't bother to call. He knew that Sven was never doing anything, so he stopped by whenever he felt like it. Usually Sven welcomed his visits, but he felt like being alone tonight.

Sven pulled on an old woolen sweater that his wife had knit him for Christmas many years ago and walked out into his front room to answer the door. Instead of Arne he saw Stephanie, all bundled up, standing at his door. She looked behind herself and then went flying off his steps and into the park.

Then he saw a man go running after her.

Sven knew it must be the man who had battered her. He was trying to catch her and beat her up again.

Sven had to help her.

Don't think. Just do it.

He put on his parka, pulled on his wool stocking hat, and lunged out the door. He could barely make out the two figures, running down toward the lake.

Sven turned and grabbed the implement that he had left standing next to the door after he had done his sidewalk—a long-handled instrument with a heavy, thick blade on the end—the ice chipper.

When Claire arrived at Stephanie's house, it looked bad. Battered, broken door, window shattered, blood on the door frame. And a horrible howling coming from inside the house.

Claire's heart stopped for a moment, and she wanted to sink to her knees and scream, but she knew she had to get into the house, no matter what she might find. She reached out to open the door and found it locked. Keeping her gloves on to preserve prints if possible, she overturned a large box that was next to the door, stood on it, reached her hand inside the door, and managed to flip the lock.

Stepping into the house, she pulled her gun out and had it at the ready. Nothing much had happened inside the house. Everything looked pretty orderly. She continued to hear the high, keening sound coming from one of the back rooms. As she stepped into the hallway, she saw that the back door was flung wide open. What the hell was going on here?

She walked slowly down the hallway, and the sound stopped. That scared her even more. Again it came, and she pushed open one of the bedroom doors. The sound was coming from the closet. Oh, God, she hated opening closets. She had seen some horrible sights.

She held her gun ready, pushed the door open with her foot, and gave a yelp of relief. The dog. The howling sound stopped, and Snooper barked up at her. He was contained in a big wire crate, and he was pawing frantically at the side of it.

"Snooper, you scared the bejezus out of me. I think you're right where you should be."

Claire closed the door again and looked in the other room. Nothing. The house didn't look disturbed. Snooper howled again, but she didn't have time to fuss with him. She needed to find Stephanie.

She ran to the back door and followed the tracks out of the door and around the house. Claire assumed they were Stephanie's. She had walked around the house and then cut down to the driveway. Claire found the tracks at the end of the driveway, but now there were two sets of footprints.

Why was she doing this to him? Jack wondered as he ran. Didn't she know he had come to explain everything to her? After the cop came this afternoon, he saw he had to keep Stephanie close by him. He saw what he always came back to: they needed to be together. It was above and beyond everything else. They had been brought together by their parents. They were born for each other. It was preordained. No one would ever love her the way he did. Why was she running away from him?

He was having trouble keeping up with her. He had been in such a hurry that he hadn't changed out of his good clothes. His fine Italian shoes were slipping in the snow. He could get no traction. He could see Stephanie ahead of him, but she just wouldn't let him get close enough to talk to her.

That's all he wanted. That's all he ever wanted was to talk to her. But she would twist everything up. She could make him so mad.

Through the falling snow, he could see a light in the trees, and he guessed that out farther was the lake. She was running toward the lake. What was she doing? The storm seemed to be centered over the lake, blowing up huge gusts of raging snow, billowing up like hands reaching out of the whiteness. His face was burning from the startling bite of the snow.

She had stopped at the edge of the lake, and he was gaining on her. He put on a burst of speed, came up behind her, and grabbed her. To have her in his hands felt so good. He would be in control soon. He swung her around, and just as he did, he felt something hit his right shoulder, a glancing blow.

"What the hell—" He spun around and saw a tall older man wielding a long stick with a blunt metal blade on one end, some sort of medieval contraption.

Without giving the man a chance to think, Jack moved in on him. He went right for the stick and yanked it out of his hands.

"No, Jack!" Stephanie screamed. "Leave him be."

What did the old guy think he was doing? Coming between him and Stephanie. He would teach him a thing or two. Then, like it always happened, he felt his rage rip through his body. It gave him so much. More strength than he knew what to do with. He saw the old man, but he saw his father, he saw all that was keeping him and Stephanie apart, and the hate that poured through him was pure and clean. He would get him this time. He would stop him for good. No one would ever tell him what to do again.

He swung the chopper at the old man as he turned to run away. The man dropped to the snow. He stayed sitting for a moment and then fell backward.

Stephanie grabbed onto Jack and tried to pull him away, but he was not to be stopped. It was too much. Interference. He threw her off him. She needed to let him do this. It would be one less thing in their way. He had the power to end it.

Jack raised the chopper up high in the air. Stephanie screamed. The snow fell all around them. Like the snow, with the weight of all the world, the chopper fell on the old man, again and again.

24

HE wind was lashing the huge branches of the cotton-
wood trees that lined the lakefront. Stephanie had always been afraid of those trees in a bad wind. They were
brittle and lost branches easily. The branches fell from such a
great distance they could do real damage—the least of her
worries now. She ran under them and out onto the lake,
where the wind was sweeping the snow up in to the air.

She couldn't stop running. She knew Jack was close behind her. She thought, for a brief crazy moment, of trying to
run across the lake. It was about a mile and a half across and
she couldn't see the lights from Lake City in this storm, so
she could easily lose her way. What she needed to do was to
get him out onto the ice and then run around him and get
back to town.

But he headed her off. He figured out what she was trying
to do and cut between her and the shore.

"Stephanie, don't do this. Stop. We can talk. Come on,
baby."

She faced him and shouted back. "Leave me alone. I hate you, you killer. You killed Sven. You killed Buck."

He stopped and screamed, "It was all for you. They were getting in between us. Don't you see? You know we have to be together."

"But why did you have to kill Buck?"

Jack looked wild in the wind, his long wool coat open and blowing off him. "He wanted it. After I told him about us, he said he didn't want to have anything to do with you. He said things about you. I had to get rid of him. Don't you see?"

Stephanie didn't want to believe him. He polluted everything he came near. She tried to run past him, and he grabbed her. His hand seemed to come out of the storm. She had circled too close to him, and he got hold of her jacket. She bent and twirled under him, kicking and punching at him as she spun, but he held on.

She tried to unzip the jacket, but couldn't get the zipper to work. Jack grabbed at her face, and she bit his hand.

Somehow she knew this would be their last fight. It had come down to this whirling in the white snow out on the frozen lake—he would kill her or she would kill him—one of them would not walk back to shore.

He was lunging at her, both hands going for her throat, when he slipped. Down he went, his knees cracking the ice underneath the snow.

She ran.

She could make out the vague outline of the trees in the light from the park. She followed the shoreline, which lifted up slightly from the flat white surface of the lake.

Suddenly she knew what she would do. Sven had warned her about a spring along the edge of the park, close to where the pier was in summer, out by the point. He said not to go over there, that the ice was weak there all winter long with the warmer springwater bubbling up. It formed a slick of glare ice. She would lead Jack over there.

She would lead him to the spring, and they would both break through the ice. She didn't care if she died anymore. She just wanted to get rid of him. To stop him.

He was close behind her again. Her breath was coming jaggedly, her lungs torn up by the cold. She didn't know how much longer she could last. The end of the point was close. She kept running. She had an idea of where the weak spot was, but in this near blind-out whiteness, she would have to guess.

Stephanie heard him getting close. The point was on her right. She knew the spring was close to shore. She cut slightly away and veered back, hoping to make him run right across it, cutting straight to get her. There was still a small part of her that hoped to get away from him.

The sound was what hit her first. A deep crack, a shriek of ice tearing apart, and then a splash and a roar from Jack. The ice sank beneath her feet, and she sunk into the freezing water, the burning-cold shock of it—cold searing through her, sucking her in. First her down jacket ballooned up around her, then as it absorbed water, it clung and pulled on her, dragging her down.

Her hands clutched the edge of the ice, and she tried to kick her way up onto the shelf. With her head above water, she felt like her body was cut off from the neck down—total paralysis. She had to force herself to move her limbs, to try to keep some warmth in her core.

"Help, Stephanie. Help me!" Jack yelled. He was in the water behind her.

Her name, now he used her name. She turned around, still holding onto the ice ledge, and kicked at him. He backed off.

When she tried to boost herself up onto the ice, the ledge broke off. She felt something on her back. Jack was grabbing her. He was trying to climb her. Utter panic and pure hate flowed through her with the cold. She decided to take him down. She swallowed a deep breath and flung her arms up in the air, sinking into the water. Jack released her, and she kicked back up to the surface.

It was then she knew she would die. They would die together. Just what Jack had always wanted.

Jack was in total panic. He was thrashing, grabbing at the edge, trying desperately to get out of the cold water. Stephanie moved away from him to the other side of the hole and found some sturdier ice toward shore, which held her weight, her arms resting on the ledge, allowing her to catch her breath.

She tried to kick her way out of the water, but again the ice broke under her weight. She fell back into the water, her head going under. When she came up, the cold had a tight hold of her. She could hardly move.

Then, suddenly, she had no more. She couldn't fight. The cold was beyond her. She gave in to it and felt herself sinking.

Claire followed the tracks as they led her down to town. They were being filled in by snow, but she could still make out the blurred outlines, the smudges they left through the white. They led her to Sven Slocum's house. But then there were many prints.

The screen door was closed, but the inner door was open at Sven's. Not a good way to keep the heat in. She stuck her head in and hollered, "Sven."

No answer. He must have joined in the chase. She turned and saw that the trail led down to the lake. She turned and ran, following the tracks.

The oddest sensation came over her as she ran. She felt like she was running in slow motion, the snow pulling at her feet. The scene was surreal: a fairy world falling in the faint light at the end of the park. But she ran faster: she hated to think of Sven getting in between John Klaus and Stephanie. No good could come of it.

She heard some voices, and then she saw the black hole in the ice. The spring. Sven had warned everyone about it. Two forms were floundering in the water. Stephanie was hanging onto the edge of the ice, and Jack was trying to grab onto her.

Claire got down on her hands and knees and started to crawl toward the hole in the lake. Jack made a feeble attempt of grabbing at Stephanie again, and she kicked him away. Then all movement stopped.

"Stephanie," Claire called. She was about five yards away from the hole. She saw a stick lying next to the hole and grabbed it. "Stephanie," she yelled louder.

A white face turned in the water. Claire didn't want to lose her. She got within a yard of the hole. The ice was holding.

"Grab onto this." She shoved the stick in front of the face. She hit Stephanie in the face, and hands instinctively came up to protect it. They grabbed the stick.

"Hold on." She dug her heels into the ice and started to pull Stephanie to the edge of the ice.

Then she heard the sound that she had heard before—a screech, a snarl of ice breaking, and the ice gave away beneath her.

The water was colder than ever, rushing around her, but she didn't go completely under. Beyond cold, she couldn't help letting out a shriek as she fell. She managed to keep her face above water.

She was afraid this time she would drown. She grabbed Stephanie around the neck, trying to stay up, trying to kick with her booted feet. She reached for the edge of the ice.

For a moment, she thought she could get out of the water. The ice felt thick beneath her hands. But she didn't know how she would manage to lift Stephanie out. The woman had gone limp in her arms. The coldness of the water crushed her. Claire felt like she couldn't breathe, could hardly move.

As she tried to hoist herself up onto the ice, it broke beneath her arm, and she plunged back into the water. She went under the surface and kicked to come back up. She still had an arm around Stephanie, but her weight dragged on Claire, making it more difficult to stay afloat.

Claire knew she didn't have long. She knew that hypothermia would set in any time now. She had to resist the urge to thrash around in the water, just to keep warm. Her mind was starting to race as she desperately tried to come up with any way out of this ice water.

She had to make an attempt at the ice. She thought of letting go of Stephanie. She would do Stephanie no good if she drowned with her. At least, if she could get herself out, she could try to rescue Stephanie. But she clung to the other woman as if she were a life jacket.

Once again, she grabbed onto the ice ledge that circled the hole. She took a deep breath and allowed herself to sink into the water. Then she kicked her legs, pushed up with her one arm, and managed to get her body partway onto the ice.

She lay there, panting, for a moment. She knew she had to let go of Stephanie to get completely onto the ice. She was afraid if she let go, Stephanie would sink into the water.

A hand grabbed her wrist.

She screamed.

"Claire."

Her name. She recognized the voice. It was Scott.

"We're here. Me and Billy. I've got you. Keep hold of her, and we'll pull you up."

Claire tightened her hold on Stephanie. They had a chance. She was starting to shake, but had to hold on.

The hand on her wrist pulled, and she felt herself being lifted onto the ice. She kept a tight hold on Stephanie. They pulled again, and she felt hands around her. Her eyes were freezing shut. She was cold beyond belief.

25

H E died with the first blow." Dr. Lord looked at Claire with his steady blue eyes, then bent his head down to cut off another piece of his pie. He had chosen apple, because it was fresh out of the oven. "The rest didn't matter."

Claire could tell he was shaken about Sven Slocum. The body had been a bloody mess when they had brought it in.

Everyone in Fort St. Antoine was very upset. People talked of little else. Sandy Polanski had posted in the post office the obituary of Sven that had run in the St. Paul paper. His children were asking that donations be made to the Women's Shelter in Durand.

Hard to believe that another nice older man had been killed in Fort St. Antoine. However, at least this time the killer was an outsider, a Minnesotan, not one of their own.

"I'm going to miss him," Claire said. "The town is going to miss him. The ice rink has drifted over with snow. He was more than a decent man, he was a good neighbor."

"High praise."

"It is around here."

Dr. Lord took a sip of his coffee. "It sounds like you're trying to become an unofficial member of the Polar Bear Club. Swimming twice in Lake Pepin in the middle of winter." Dr. Lord laughed as he said it. He bent his head and cut off another piece of his apple pie.

Claire gave him a glare over her cup of coffee. "It took me all night to thaw out from that dip."

"You were very lucky that help was so close at hand."

"I hate to think about it."

"So you were going to tell me what happened to the guy that did all this? Klaus?"

"Yes, John Klaus is his name. Just moved him to the jail. He suffered severe frostbite to his feet. He was wearing the thinnest shoes you can imagine—they had to amputate a couple of his toes. He was in the water a lot longer. First Scott and Billy got Stephanie and me into the warm car. Then they went back for Klaus."

Dr. Lord's eyes grew wider behind his glasses. "And this all happened the night of the storm?"

Claire nodded. "We could tell Stephanie was okay. She didn't want to go back to Durand, so she stayed with me that night. Scott and Billy drove Klaus back to Durand at the full height of the storm. Then they both ended up staying the night there. I think they slept in a couple of the jail cells. Once there, they couldn't leave. But at least we didn't need to keep Klaus at my house all night."

"So you know for sure that Klaus killed Buck Owens?"

"Yeah. He told Stephanie. His wife admitted that she didn't know where he had been that night. Oh, I didn't tell you. He had left her at home with a broken arm and a bruised face." Claire looked out the window. Overcast, but not too cold outside. They hadn't had any snow since the big storm. "We've got him on two murder counts. And the assault of Stephanie Klaus. If there were a death penalty in Wisconsin, he'd be a candidate."

"And his tie with Stephanie Klaus?"

"Legally they were siblings, but they'd been lovers for many years. Nothing wrong with that, again legally. However, because they were raised as siblings, it's a little weird. According to her, he had been beating her up for most of that time. Once she started talking, it all poured out of her."

"Well, the good news is that Stephanie has done what she needs to do." He pointed his fork at Claire, but she didn't take it personally. "She came through this thing alive. Too many women get killed by their abusers."

"But I think she feels awful about Sven. She kept saying that night that she hadn't even asked him in for a cup of coffee when he dropped her off from the hospital." Claire thought of her dead husband for a moment. "Sometimes that's all you want—just the chance to have another cup of coffee with them."

When the bell rang, Meg shouted a silent hurrah in her mind. School was finally over for this year. She wouldn't be back in this classroom until after the New Year. But she couldn't leave right away. Mr. Turner had asked Meg to stay for a moment after school was out. She had all the stuff she needed to take home with her piled on top of her desk. Two weeks of vacation. Her mom was even going to take a few days off to hang out with her. What fun.

She wasn't too worried about Mr. Turner anymore. He was letting her read when she finished her work and had even told her her last project on Wisconsin state history had been excellent. She had written a report on the Chippewa, or Ojibwa, Indians. They had lived in Fort St. Antoine before the people from Europe came and pushed them off their land. She had once found an arrowhead down at the park. It was a soft pink color. She kept it in her collection of special things in a box next to her bed, and had drawn a picture of it for her report. He had liked the picture; most of the other kids hadn't illustrated their reports.

But as she watched the other kids leave the room, she got a bad feeling. She looked up at Mr. Turner. He was taking his time, wiping down the board. What would he do to her now? Something to ruin her vacation?

He turned around and walked back toward her desk. His face was scrunched up as if he were making it a point to look like he was thinking. He really looked more like he had a fly on his nose and was trying to look at it. He stood above her for a few moments before saying anything. Meg got a sick feeling in her stomach.

"Meg, I've read your story. The fairy tale you turned in for extra credit. You have a very vivid imagination. When the princess pushed the monster out onto the ice and he fell through, I was quite surprised."

She nodded. She was pretty pleased with how that had turned out.

"The reason I asked you to wait is . . . I think it's quite good."

Meg felt relieved. Was that all?

Mr. Turner sat down in the desk in front of her. It felt weird to be at the same level with him. She could see that he was getting wrinkles on his forehead.

"I just wanted to let you know how happy I am that you have come to see things my way."

Meg decided he could think that if he wanted to. She got to read in class whenever she was done with her homework. She got to write stories that she made up for extra credit. She felt like she was getting everything she wanted from school. She wasn't going to argue with him about whose idea it was.

"Thanks, Mr. Turner." She stood up and picked up her books. She had a bus to catch. "I'm going to try to write another one over Christmas. Is that all?"

"That would be fine, Meg." Mr. Turner seemed to shrink as she stood there. His shoulders sagged, and he looked a little bit lonely. She wondered what he was doing for the holi-days

Meg started to leave, and then turned back and said, "Have a merry Christmas, Mr. Turner."

His voice followed her out the door. "You too, Meg."

Beatrice saw the town of Fort St. Antoine come in sight, then they drove right by Rich's farmhouse and on to his girl-friend's. What an odd thing to call a woman in her forties—a girlfriend. They really had to come up with a better word: companion, mistress, or even compatriot. It was a week be-fore Christmas, and Beatrice had been invited over to deco-rate the tree at Claire's house.

Beatrice had decided that she would not make them put up with her this Christmas Eve or day. Let them have that time together without the old woman there. She had good friends in Rochester who had begged her to come and have dinner with them. There might be other Christmases that she could share with her son when he was more settled with this new arrangement. If it lasted.

When she walked in the door of Claire's house, she was struck by how warm and pleasant it felt. A fire going in the woodstove, a sliced fruitcake sitting on the coffee table, a bot-tle of wine opened and at the ready.

Claire brushed her cheek with her own, pleasant but a lit-tle distant. However, Meg hugged her around the waist and reached up to give her a kiss. Beatrice could see no way out of it, so she bent over slowly and received the kiss, like a touch of a snowflake, on her cheek.

Beatrice had brought over a wrapped present for Meg and Claire. She handed it to Meg after their greetings.

"May I open it?" Meg asked.

Beatrice nodded.

"Now?"

"The sooner the better."

Meg tore off the wrapping paper, and her mouth grew round and her eyes widened as she lifted the tissue paper off the prettiest blown-glass ornament that Beatrice could find—a swirl of soft pastels.

"For the tree?" Meg asked.

"Unless you want to wear it in your hair."

Claire looked at the gift. "It will be the very first ornament we put on the tree. I will find it a place of honor."

Claire gave Beatrice a shy hug and handed her a glass of wine, showing her to a spot on the couch from where she could watch the tree-trimming with ease.

"Hey?" Meg said to her.

"Straw is cheaper," Beatrice said back.

Meg looked blankly at her, then her face broke into a smile as she got the joke. "Good one."

"What, Meg?"

"Beatrice, that bulb you gave us is a real flower now. Come and see it."

Meg took her hand and led her into the kitchen. There on a shelf next to the window, but out of the light, as she had told them, was the amaryllis "Picotee," looking as lovely as it could look: a long dusky green stem rising up a good foot and a half with four huge blossoms facing the four directions.

"A white ghost of a flower with just a hint of red," she said to Meg.

"It will still be blooming on Christmas Day, don't you think?" Meg asked.

"Yes. Now, Meg, when the flowers die back, then you cut the stem off, but let the leaves grow. Keep watering it. I'll tell you what to do with it in spring." Beatrice stopped as she realized she sounded as if she was sure this relationship would last. She hoped it would. She placed her hand on Meg's dark hair. "If you treat it right, you should have this flower blooming at Christmas for many years to come."

✦

When the stars faded behind her eyes, she opened them and saw Rich's face close to hers. Handsome man. He sniffed her neck as if he still hadn't gotten enough of her. She bent her head and found his lips and kissed him. She stretched in his arms, and he held her tight.

"That was positively celestial," she whispered.

"So close to Christmas I do my best."

"I'll have to remember that."

"I'm good on all the holidays."

"After New Year's there's Ground Hog Day."

He snuffled harder into her neck, sounding like a wild animal. "Don't forget Boxing Day and President's Day."

Claire pulled herself up in bed and cradled Rich's head in her arms. "I don't have to work tomorrow."

"That's a reason to celebrate in itself. That job has been taking a lot out of you lately."

She didn't say anything. She had noticed that he had started to snipe a bit about her work, hinting that she might think of doing something else. It wasn't a good sign. It hadn't helped at all that he had been there to see Stephanie Klaus after she was beaten. It had given him too strong a sense of what her job was all about. She might need to nip his concern in the bud. He didn't have as much to keep him busy in the winter, and he had too much time to think about what she was doing.

"The job is fine. It's a lot easier down here in Pepin than it was up in the big, bad cities."

"You seemed a little upset when you came home from work today," he said, pulling himself up next to her.

"Oh, yeah. I didn't want to say anything with Meg around. I didn't get a chance to show it to you, but I read a story that she wrote the other day. It was really excellent. She's turning into quite a writer. But there was a dark side to it. I know that isn't unusual with kids. But it worries me that she might be hearing too much about what I'm working on."

"Meg's growing up. I think she can handle it. I think you

just need to keep putting it in perspective. There is evil, and there is good. Just think of what's on TV, in the newspaper. You can't keep the world from her."

"Yeah, I guess."

"So what happened today?" he asked again, wrapping an arm around her back as if protecting her from what she was about to tell him.

Claire sighed. "Maybe it means nothing. I wish I could believe that. But I was leaving work, and as I was walking down the steps, I saw Stephanie Klaus park her car. I got into my car and then watched as she walked up the steps of the jailhouse and went in. She went into the jailhouse, Rich. She had to be going in to see John Klaus. After all he's done to her."

Rich rubbed Claire's back and shoulders. He could feel her tense up just talking about it. "Any addiction is hard to get over. Whatever they have is like an addiction to both of them."

"Should I have said something to her? Stopped her? Reminded her of what she looked like when we found her on Thanksgiving? Isn't it my job to stop this kind of thing from happening again?"

"I don't think so. You have done your job. He's in jail. He will be convicted. He will go away for the rest of his life. That's where your job ends. You can't save everybody, Claire."

There was one more thing, but she didn't tell Rich. She wasn't sure why. It twisted inside her, and she didn't even want to say it out loud. Stephanie had been carrying a present in her hands. It was all wrapped up in Christmas wrapping paper with a big red bow.

Printed in the United States
By Bookmasters